welcome to
BREEZEWOOD

welcome to

BREEZEWOOD

DAVID STURM

DEVIL'S PARTY PRESS, MILTON, DE

WELCOME TO BREEZEWOOD

TO MY WIFE, LAURIE

D.S.

welcome to
BREEZEWOOD

1

Crows are the felons of the bird world. Common thieves, opportunistic alley lurkers, merciless even to sparrow fledglings in a nest, a peeping wad of protein they will scoop up and hork down while the sparrow parents flap around in pathetic protest. They are Audubon's sociopaths—seagulls being their only possible rivals in search and seizure.

Is it good for crows? That's the only corvine filter. For these omnivorous birds, there are no rules. Food is all. And, making more crows. There aren't many crow enemies, but these creatures are still on the lookout for trouble. If you are a bird, best make peace with the crows.

Here they were now, a pack of black-cloaked malefactors looking for a best chance.

Atop a towering white pine in southcentral Pennsylvania, this flock of crows roosted, waiting for evening to fall. The black conspirators regarded each other like drunken priests in a Boston pub. They have plenty on each other. A collection of owls is a parliament; for crows, a murder.

One adjusted its perch and gave its wings a flap, drawing a caw in rebuke from another, which also refolded itself. Ruffling aside, the crows were settling in for the night. This is their permanent home, even in winter, because these stoic birds, annealed by hardship, do not migrate north or south. The North American crow does not complain and does not explain. It simply takes a grip on what it needs to survive and doesn't let go. As far as the crow is concerned, you can go to hell. All you can do for the crow is get out of its way.

This white pine is a slight anomaly amid the oaks, hickories, and other hardwoods of piedmont Pennsylvania. An advantage, at least to the crows, to this particular long-needled tree, is that perching here provides them with a vantage over a road directly below that cuts through the forest, leaving a swath on either side of the asphalt. The roadside occasionally yields carrion of various kinds or cold french fries tossed from a passing car. The passing below of humans is good for crows.

Even better, when dawn breaks the crows drop to the asphalt and poke through the weeds, grass, and wet leaves on either side to gorge on the plump slugs that emerge with the morning dew.

With the coming of winter, the crow lives by endurance, observation, and wits. The slightest rustle in the underbrush triggers the predator impulse and the bird swoops, claws out, for the scurrying field mouse. Glamour-puss predators like red-tailed hawks, ospreys, and eagles get the spotlight, but the lowborn crow hustles its living by leaving its low-rent options open. It knows the locations of human dwellings, where uncovered garbage is always a feast. After a day of grifting, from both creatures that mourn and those that don't even notice, the black birds return to their lofty pine and stretch their necks to give up their unmelodic cough, demanding that the world acknowledge their corvine superiority.

As the shadows lengthen here, the birds' curiosity is drawn to an embankment on the other side of the road where a man sits eating a sandwich. The spot could be a place to forage in the morning. The food possibilities in warm weather are ridiculously abundant for creatures gifted with wings, memory, and an appetite for anything with caloric value, from pizza crusts to hatchlings. The crows are willing to wait, always alert for a mistake by some weaker element. Foolish behavior can yield a bounty. Caloric value. That covered for a lot of depravity if calculated on a certain scale.

On the embankment below the white pine, Harold tossed what was left of his hamburger in the grass and licked the fat from his fingers.

What happened to my handkerchief? Harold wondered, unable to remember. A bigger issue, the burger was not sitting right in his gullet. *Wish I had a Tanqueray and tonic, or even a beer.* His shoulders slumped. Either drink would probably tie a knot in his stomach and fill his armpits with sweat. What the hell was wrong with his guts?

An impossible task loomed: escape. But maybe not impossible. Sitting on the grass with his back against a chain-link fence surrounding an electrical substation, he took stock. No one was in sight and the only sound was the thrum of traffic on Interstate 70 behind him on the ridge uphill. From where he sat, he couldn't be seen from the highway.

His car? Funny you should ask. It was kaput, maybe a blown gasket—he just drove it, he didn't know or care how it worked—now parked on a dirt access road that led to a utility tower behind a brace of trees to his left. He left the keys in the Porsche. Piece of French shit. *Au revoire, mon pire ennemi.* He was about one hundred yards from the Boxter as darkness enfolded.

Night was imminent. He burped from the hamburger, his suit pants were soaked from the grass, and he didn't know what to do next except stay out of sight.

What was the endgame of this going to be? If he could figure out the last chapter, he'd know what to do next. He simply could not summon the outcome of this caper. He liked that word, caper. He saw himself in an Alfred Hitchcock movie, a raffish scamp fleeing the authorities. He would redeem himself and win over a flustered Audrey Hepburn before the end credits. Sure.

He needed a plan.

He laughed out loud. *Isn't that what everyone said when the situation was as absurd as this? What's that Jewish saying about men planning and God laughing?*

Still, Harold might have some time, and with time he might find a break. He remembered stories of the guys who got away. There was D.B. Cooper, a skyjacker who parachuted from a 727 with $200,000. Harold would have to summon his wits to a degree he never had before. All he needed was that parachute. If there was a way out of this, he'd find it, even without a parachute. Still, Harold clung to the idea of a parachute.

Bail out with the loot!

Well, except he didn't have the loot. Or a parachute. Or even a fucking car. And he was sitting on the grass in the dark. And his clothes were wet.

Two things happened.

First, blue and red flashing lights appeared behind the brace of trees.

The cops had found his car.

Second, a lazy whup-whup sound grew in intensity until Harold realized a helicopter was approaching. In a panicked sweat, he burst from him and he scrambled to his feet. He raced through the high grass to the tree line and bolted into a patch of woods just as the helicopter thundered overhead, shining a spotlight where he had just been sitting. Harold reached into his pocket and found his cellphone, glaring accusingly at the treacherous device in his palm. He didn't really know if the phone had betrayed him, but he threw it as far as he could.

No choice now. He had to move. As always, downhill looked best. He pulled his wet pants and underwear out of his ass crack and braced himself to plunge through dewy grass to what lay below. The overhead canopy of darkness and trees closed in. Overcast skies obscured the moon and Harold saw that he would soon be engulfed in cave-like darkness. Water from the wet grass was now gathering in his shoes, which made a spongy sound as he walked. The insects were coming into full throat. Trilling locusts were the soundtrack to his soggy downhill progress.

This was far from what he had anticipated when he first considered his intention to get bent. Arrest? Maybe. But lost in the woods?

The slope descended to an unlit rural road with no apparent traffic at this hour. Darkness in all directions. He scanned as far as he could. Right or left? If he turned right, he would continue in the direction he had been headed on I-70. He turned right, embarking on a steady walk along the shoulder. The annoyance with the turmoil in his crotch grew with each step.

He reached into his right pants pocket and tickled the flash drive. His ticket. He felt a little better.

Gravel crunched underfoot. Harold tried to summon a map of southcentral Pennsylvania that would give him a clue of where he might be. No luck. He had not an inkling of where he walked. No road

signs, just trees, in sight. It seemed he was walking down a trough with
an asphalt bottom and tree-lined sides. An American two-lane blacktop stretching to God knew where. All he could do was put one foot
in front of the other.

Behind him suddenly…headlights.

A vehicle lying in wait abruptly announcing its sinister presence
but not approaching. Not yet. Distantly, he heard the engine *harrumph*
to life. He'd been discovered. To the authorities now, he was the prey.
Which authority was it? It hardly mattered. He'd simply be passed up
the chain to whatever agency could inflict upon him the most damage.

Or, was it some local udder squeezer making a milk delivery?
This was, after all, rural Pennsylvania. Someone smoking a cheap cigar
and watching the fuel tank level as he hauled cans of moo juice.

No.

He was a target. He was sure of it. To think otherwise was
surely a mistake.

The car, truck, SUV, pickup, or whatever, was a quarter mile
back. It would close the distance in less than a minute.

Harold ran now.

He could hardly be wearing more unsuitable clothes for a run—
Black Ferragamo loafers and a Brooks Brothers suit. Might as well be
chain mail and boots of sponge. He glanced quickly to his left and
right. He could plunge into the trees on either side and begin clawing
his way uphill. The panic of exertion began to inflame Harold's lungs.
Rivulets of sweat coursed down his torso. He had never felt this wet
without swimming.

Then, ahead, he saw a highway crossing. Gasping, he reached
the berm of the six-lane road and paused. Harold spent a few precious
seconds to calm his heaving chest.

Speeding tires on a wet street coursed in two directions across
his path. Speeding tires on the wet street made a wheezing sound like
a choking man gasping for breath. Headlights, reflected on greasy asphalt, illuminated nothing useful. A slipstream of sound and light
crossed his path.

He had to cross.

There was no red signal, just a stop sign for traffic in his direction. He had to make a dash. Harold looked backward. The vehicle
behind him was closing in relentlessly.

The chess clock ran down. The oven timer dinged. The bugle

blew. Time to move.

A semi bore down on his left, tires frothing the water on the highway, and traffic hung back behind it. As soon as the semi and the cars trailing it rocketed past, Harold leapt. He wanted to cross three lanes so he could stop, then confront traffic coming the other way from the safe center line. He had never seriously dodged through heavy traffic, but he was fit and, at least, sober.

But he misjudged from the start. A car barreling up the far left lane intent on passing the semi had just crossed behind. Harold saw a gap and leaped forward. He crossed two lanes but had not anticipated the passing car in the last lane. He might have outraced it.

At that moment the toe-caressing calfskin and daringly tasseled upper of his Ferragamos proved useless as the slick leather sole slid on the wet, oily asphalt. His right foot leapt upward in front of him like he was punting a ball, and his left knee buckled.

He was abruptly helpless, with legs unable to keep him balanced and erect.

The approaching driver didn't even honk. No time. The only sound above the traffic noise was the squeal of brakes as the car slewed sideways to the right. He saw the driver, a long-haired teenager, mouth agape in incomprehension, staring at this tipped-sideways character as the driver's side of the car hurtled at him. The vehicle was a two-ton swinging door and Harold was sprawled in the doorway, trapped in the path of hurtling steel with a baffled teenager at the wheel.

The impact bounced him.

He felt his legs and hips rearrange instantly into something unrecognizable, attachments without any sane connection to his body that flipped above his head. He was upside down in mid-air, a tossed ragdoll.

Harold saw the roof of the car pass beneath him. Then he was going down and he saw the asphalt rise to meet his face. Upon impact, his head twisted to the side and he sensed teeth and mandible loosening. He was vaguely aware of the rest of his body flopping down like a dropped sack of clattering bones. Recoil sent Harold rolling from front to back. He opened his eyes and glimpsed stars as he painfully heaved air into his lungs. *But how could there be stars?* he wondered. *It was cloudy after the rain.* The stars vanished and only darkness remained as consciousness snapped off.

2

It remained night on a wet rural road, but traffic was now absent. The summer evening air carried the thick weight of the previous day's heat and was filled with the sounds of insects and frogs. The woods still encroached, and the heavy presence of recent rain still prevailed. Warm weather nights in Penn's Woods.

Lights appeared and shimmered on the wet asphalt. A lone set of headlights wobbled into view in the distance.

Behind the lights a motor coughed. Poor suspension made the lights jog a bit, throwing out jagged illumination. But the six-volt single contact headlamps nonetheless picked up something in the middle of the road.

A squealing sound of stripped brakes signaled an attempt to stop. And, eventually, stop it did, keeping the pool of light on a man splayed in the middle of the road in a way that looked like he ought to be outlined in chalk.

Within the truck, mild consternation. The obstacle could be easily removed to a ditch, but some obligation arose, if only theoretically, if the body turned out to be a human being in extremis. After all, this could be someone recognizable to someone else. Information had its uses.

Harold Worthington's eyes snapped open.

He sucked in air and tried to make sense out of what loomed over him. The faces of two men. He flexed his body in a probe for pain. Only his head. He touched his forehead and looked at his hand. Blood. But not a spate, just a trickle. He had made it. Somehow. And here he was, supine on a blacktop road. What miracles awaited next?

The faces remained overhead. One of them scratched beneath his chin with a fingernail.

This one, who Harold would learn was Max, had a shaved face except for a pencil moustache that sat like a plucked eyebrow over his upper lip. He wore a bowler hat tilted to the side. The other, Benny, was fully bearded. They were both dressed like swells whose fortunes had been reduced in the Charlie Chaplin era.

Benny whispered to Harold, "Are we being watched?"

Harold's mind tried to devise an answer. *Maybe. Who knows? Why ask?* "I don't think so," he croaked.

It was Max's turn. "Who dumped you here? Was it the Hunkie? That unholy bastard!"

Harold wanted to give an account and searched his memory. Nobody dumped him. It wasn't the Hunkie, whoever that was. His eyes clamped shut and he came up with the answer. He opened his eyes. *Tell the truth. What the hell.*

"A car hit me."

"You were out here taking a stroll at night?"

"I was running away from someone."

Well, an answer that made sense. The two men straightened up to confer.

Benny said, "Blotto?"

"Can't say. Probably, some poor sap."

Some unspoken agreement was reached. Each man took one of Harold's arms and they pulled Harold to his feet. Harold staggered, but steadied himself as he began to walk. With the men's hands under each armpit, he had no choice but to follow to—what is this?—a truck that belonged in a sepia photo parked in front of a dry goods emporium on the teeming Lower East Side.

Benny opened the passenger door and shouldered Harold into

the cab, shoving him toward the center of a wooden bench. He climbed inside and shut the door. Max got in and turned the ignition key. The engine snorted to life. Max pressed down a clutch, which made a clunking sound, and shoved a gearshift the size of a golf club into first gear. He eased up the clutch and the whole array lurched forward. Two more shifts and the truck hit an easy roll.

Harold realized the two men had no further curiosity about him. They hadn't even asked his name.

He examined the cab. It had no dashboard, just a vertically aligned windshield. The steering wheel was on a post practically extending out of the floor. All three of them sat on a wooden bench. Harold looked up. Over the windshield a rack held a shotgun. He looked at Benny, whose leather vest was propped open, revealing a Smith & Wesson .32 caliber in a shoulder holster.

Max chewed a toothpick as he drove while Benny cleaned his fingernails with a penknife. Two armed men going about their business in an antique truck in the middle of the night. Perhaps not a milk run. Perhaps an element of danger here.

Harold cleared his throat. "Where are we?"

They both lazily swung their gaze at him.

"Step right up, folks. It walks. It talks," Benny finally said.

"C'mon, man," Harold said.

Benny tilted his head. "Flyspeck you never heard of on Lincoln Highway called Breezewood. We have to make a delivery."

"Where's the Interstate?"

This drew winces.

Benny removed his toothpick. "Are you familiar with a state called Pennsylvania?"

"Sure, but I just don't know …"

"You don't know from nothin', do ya, palsy walsy? Probably your brain's been addled," Max said, as Benny chuckled.

Up ahead, the tunnel of trees widened and the headlamps revealed a cleared area on the left where a gravel parking lot displayed at least twenty parked cars and pickup trucks around a low, one-story frame building with no identifying sign. Harold did a mind capture of what he was seeing in case, for whatever reason, he had to explain himself later. The data he had collected so far fit no known template. All he really could do was watch and learn.

Harold and his companions pulled into the lot and the pickup slowed to a stop with a squeal. One by one they exited.

The truck had a canvas-covered frame, and Harold followed the two men to the tailgate, which Max dropped after sliding a bolt. Harold peered inside. Wooden cases were piled up. All were labeled Canadian Club.

Benny climbed into the back and handed a case to Harold, who almost staggered under its weight.

"Don't you drop that. More pain coming your way you bust one of them bottles."

Each man carried a case each to a door, illuminated by a single light bulb that burned overhead. Max pressed a doorbell. Everyone waited.

"Who is it?" The voice was comically fluty.

"Cut the gag. You know who it is."

The voice inside trilled, "Say the password."

"Password? Kiss my Polack ass. That's the password."

Laughter erupted inside as the door opened and the three men strode in. Harold followed the other two as they thumped their cases down on a long bar.

Harold was abruptly in a place wholly at odds with the building's outdoor warehouse appearance.

It was a party. People were as lit up as the sconces on the wall of the crowded room. They shouted over half-empty glasses that littered the tables, fighting to be heard over the music, a rollicking jazz tune. Harold recognized "Muskrat Ramble."

Couples clog-danced energetically on a dance floor. The boards slammed under their rhythmic stomping and their faces turned to the ceiling in the abandonment that comes when music propels the feet. A few even did the Charleston, a wicked dance from the city. Some men sported pushed-back straw boaters while women wore cloche hats and tasseled skirts above pumping legs.

Tobacco smoke enshrouded everything in the room. Harold watched cigarettes, cigars, and pipes give up their volcanic essence.

Harold took all this in after finding a spot at the bar. He tried to make sense of it all. He scanned the crowd for a familiar connection. A Nittany Lions T-shirt, at least. Penn State wasn't that far. But no dice.

The men and women were an American cross section John Steinbeck would recognize: farmers, mechanics, salesmen, college students, and housewives out for a fling. They were all ages and races. They were all drinking and some even had bottles on their table.

How? he wondered. *How can this be?* The verisimilitude of this pageant was so vivid Harold could not process it outside of its evident authenticity. It was no dream.

But maybe he could fit all this into a template that made sense in some other way. Some kind of theater or living tableau?

At that moment, a drunken gabbling man at one table had a mug of beer poured on his head by a red-faced woman, to the uproarious reaction of the crowd. They laughed even more as he ostentatiously tried to lick the beer from his moustache. The red-faced woman threw her arms around his neck and planted a wet kiss on his ear as the man waggled his tongue. The crowd's uproar became even louder.

Next to Harold, Benny opened one of his boxes and extracted a bottle covered in paper and straw.

Up sauntered a woman of middle age in a fringed dress with Cleopatra eye makeup. She wore a headband adorned with Egyptian figures. One hand was on her hip, which was cocked, and the other held a cigarette holder with an unlit filterless Chesterfield. The bartender snapped a match and lit it for her. He whispered briefly in her ear and she lifted a hand in acknowledgement. In this place, it was clear, she had the mojo and the say-so.

She regarded Harold with some amusement.

"Who's he?"

"Some ragamuffin," Benny answered. "Found him along the road, knocked out."

She pursed her lips and lifted her eyebrows as she regarded Harold as someone who could prove useful someday, then got down to matters at hand.

"Besides him, what else did you bring me?"

Max held a bottle by the neck and lifted it like a trophy. "Lookee here, Mamie. This is the goods. Canadian. Straight from Windsor. Bonded."

"Canadians don't bond whiskey, you dope," Mamie said, with a smirk. Her voice was heavy weather.

"Well, if they did, this would be bonded."

Harold spotted a newspaper farther down the bar and retrieved it. The front bore a photo of Franklin Delano Roosevelt. Harold checked the date and his hand flew to his mouth. He felt momentarily faint. It couldn't be.

But, his gut told him, it could. And was.

"It's 1933." His head turned sideways and his eyes went up to the ceiling. "It's 1933."

He felt a jab in his ribs and turned to see a drunk on a barstool. The souse issued an exaggerated wink.

"Time of reckoning for all of us sinners," the drunk said, and downed the last of his whiskey. "Here's to 1933. A journey awaits, God knows where."

Two other men at the bar tossed theirs down in salute.

Mamie wiped the bar with a rag. "Amen, brother," she said. "So long, Hoobert Heever. Good riddance to bad rubbish."

The drunk pulled an ashtray over, tapped a Camel out of a pack, put it in the corner of his mouth, thumbed a match until it flared, and lit up. After a couple of thoughtful puffs, he pointed the cigarette at Mamie.

"We're going wet again, Mamie," he said. "FDR's all for repeal. Won't be any speaks anymore. Watcha think about that?"

"Roadhouses ain't going anywhere. I aim to stick around."

A sudden thought hit Harold and he reached into a pants pocket. The flash drive was still there. He sucked in air and blew it out slowly. He had a computer flash drive in his pocket in 1933. How do you bend your brain around that?

Harold returned his attention to the newspaper, wondering if it was a prop like he'd seen in movies. He flipped through it and saw all the pages filled with the news of the day and ads for toothache remedies, Lucky Strike cigarettes, and RCA Victor radios. On the front page he glimpsed a breathlessly written story about how a foiled assassination attempt on New Jersey Senator Charles Eaton. In another story, Jehovah's Witnesses in Germany staged a protest rally over Nazi attempts to suppress their worship. The scandal-plagued actor, Fatty Arbuckle, had died of a heart attack at age forty-six.

Harold folded the newspaper and tried to digest what he had learned. *Learned?* he thought. *What about no scars after body annihilation on the highway? What lesson is that?* He envisioned a classroom of kids waving hands in the air. "I know! I know!" He decided he preferred not to know.

The dance band wound up and left the stage. The dancers ambled, arm-in-arm or solo, some unsteadily, back to their smoke-shrouded tables. The drummer came over to a dapper black man having a drink at the bar and tapped his shoulder.

"You're on, Johnson."

The name tickled Harold's imagination. He turned to see who it was. Then, he felt his curiosity well up and even overflow.

Johnson's fedora had a rakish angle and he was sharp in a dark pinstripe double breasted with a handkerchief folded into a tube in the breast pocket. Harold looked down at the guitar propped next to Johnson's barstool. It was a Kalamazoo, the low-end line by Gibson.

Harold's mind raced. The name. The guitar. The year. *It couldn't be.*

Johnson picked up a barstool in one hand and his guitar in the other and ambled to the stage, perching himself on the stool. He tuned his guitar briefly, then turned to the crowd.

"Good evening, ladies and gents. Lemme ask you all a question. Where we at? We got two highways crossing. That makes a crossroads. Devil likes them crossroads. Wonder if that devil is here now. The lord of sin himself. Patriarch of all that badness. Mmm, mmm, mmm."

The guitarist offered a complicit grin and lowered his hat a bit over his forehead.

A whistle from the crowd rang out and Johnson offered a salute.

After a blues intro, he began to sing. "I went to the crossroads, got down on my knees ..."

Harold was transfixed. He had played this song.

His hand went into his suit jacket pocket and found, where he expected it, his Hohner. He pulled it out. He thumbed its well-rubbed surface. Metal and maple, an American match. He put the harmonica to his mouth and blew notes of backup to what Johnson was playing.

Johnson glanced his way. Harold stopped blowing, sheepish. *Stepping on an act?* Then he saw a smile from the bluesman.

And he blew again, and again, and Johnson picked out and strummed that twin guitar sound, lead and rhythm, that professional guitarists have never figured out. Harold hooted on his harp in basic accompaniment.

The song ended and Johnson gave him an appraising look, pointing at the Hohner.

"Where you learn that?"

"St. James Infirmary."

"I actually doubt that."

"Parchman Farm?"

Johnson rolled his eyes.

"Doesn't matter how I learned it. In a way, from you."

"You been to Mississippi?"

"No, man. It's a long story," Harold said. He extended a hand. "I'm Harold."

"Robert."

To Harold, the handshake was impossible, but thrillingly real. It was as real as the soiled tie, bloodshot wink, and whiskey breath of the man who stood, close up and in person, in naked blues glory before him.

Before releasing Johnson's hand, he looked down at the fingernails on the bluesman's right hand. They were cut a certain way, like a cresting wave. Fingers and nails separately on the strings. Now he knew. There were a million blues fans who would also love to know how this man cut his fingernails.

Shit, if he could take a picture of this man's fingernails and post it on the internet. He almost reached for a cellphone he no longer had.

Of course. It's 1933, so why shouldn't this be Robert Johnson in a Pennsylvania speakeasy on a highway in the middle of Iamlost, USA. Johnson was constantly on the road. The Kalamazoo balanced on his lap was the Holy Grail of instruments, forever lost. Harold realized the venerable bluesman had only five years to live before he would woo the wrong woman and be poisoned by her jealous husband. Even the whereabouts of his grave was a mystery, since headstones bearing his name have been put up in three different places.

Johnson continued his set. "Come on in My Kitchen," "Kind Hearted Woman Blues," "Love in Vain." His sharp, reedy voice finally fell on Bessie Smith's "Nobody Knows You When You're Down and Out."

The audience lit up, called to attention. It was like the sound of a distant anthem on a battlefield; those who share it know its meaning.

And they were rapt. These men in their overalls and starched shirts, women in the best dresses they could afford lowered their heads and nodded a bit as bottles were lifted and poured. Cigarettes were stubbed out. A woman stood and swayed. A salute to a new call to class consciousness at a time when the boot on the neck was barely a metaphor. One woman threw her hands up in praise and lifted her head. Heads shook back and forth in appreciation.

It occurred to Harold this was a song that simultaneously swung and bit. An American song.

The drinkers lifted their voices in the refrain.

Harold returned to the bar to find Mamie pouring him a magnificent shot.

"Any friend of Max and Benny is probably a crook," she said. "But I'll stand him to a belt."

He downed the amber liquor and let the fiery corn-and-rye distillate flow down his throat like trouble ahead. Another was poured and Harold took it to the back of the bar, where he found a hallway that led to another door. He went through and stepped out onto a back porch.

A beat-up sofa beckoned and he sat his tired ass down. His sore back gave him gratitude for this relief. He tossed back the Canadian hooch, set the glass on the boards at his feet, and laced his hands across his chest. He indulged in a deep sigh.

It was quiet. Harold realized what a blessing that was.

He was alone on the porch. Noises from inside the speakeasy were muffled to a distant purr out here. The sofa he sat on was faintly moist, but he didn't care. He had a thought that made him laugh. "Put on your thinking cap, Harold. Don't make your brain do all the work," his father always said. How, exactly, did that work in this situation? He threw his head back and closed his eyes. *C'mon, thinking cap, do a brain override.* Did he have a next move? Somehow, he had to make sense out of what was going on. *What do you do when things just. Don't. Fucking. Fit?*

Weariness engulfed Harold, and he stretched his back muscles. His entire body gave in to gravity. He closed his eyes.

———

The patter of feet approaching awakened Harold. His arms tried to find purchase to push himself up, but it was too late. Strong hands grabbed both arms and pinned him down. He blinked, trying to gain focus. He was being attacked. Two seconds passed before he realized why.

A man with a shaved head in a trench coat loomed over

Harold. The man's face was all knuckled eyes and bared teeth, and he lowered this face to take a close look at Harold, now helpless in an unrelenting grip.

He took Harold's measure like it was something pestilential needing extermination.

"It's him."

"You have …" Harold managed, before a hand slapped his face into silence.

Shaved Head gripped the front of his shirt. "Where's the flash drive?" Spittle flecked his lips, which he licked, and he arched his head backwards before returning his laser gaze on Harold. "Give me an excuse. Oh, just give me an excuse you cowardly cocksucker."

The coppery taste of blood filled Harold's mouth. He couldn't summon anything he wanted to say, much less utter it.

"Fucking traitor!"

Shaved Head drew his fist back, precursor to a blow to Harold's head.

Harold felt a moment of clarity. He was a victim of authority gone rogue, and he felt an instant of indignant righteousness before a rock encased in flesh landed. Hard. Harold's head snapped back, then, after the hands released him, he pitched forward into the uncaring forest gloom.

3

Harold lay face down in deep grass. It was pathetic. He was in the dark, face in grass, listening. No sound except the vague forest chee-chee of insects. He opened his eyes and ventured a look. Just high grass next to his face. He had to lift his head to see anything, and he did. Carefully.

Nobody this way. He turned his head. *Nobody that way.* He got his hands under his shoulders and pushed up. *Nobody. Nobody here but us chickens, in the dark, in the grass, under the trees, somewhere probably still heavily forested in a godforsaken corner of Pennsylvania.*

He moved to a sitting position and touched his face. No detectable damage.

Before him was a wrecked cabin. A gaping sinkhole had sucked down half of it, though it still had a back porch with a bench where, apparently, he had been sitting, except on a couch.

Harold straightened up. The speakeasy, the parking lot, the cars and trucks—nowhere to be seen. He was surrounded by trees and a few head-high limestone outcroppings.

He sensed the time change instantly.

It was moonless and he was in some lost-in-history spot with only a ruined cabin to indicate any human had ever been here. He drew his hand down his face. *Why?*

His clothes were sodden and how long had it been since he had eaten? Or taken a shower? Or brushed his teeth? Or shaved? Harold stroked his chin and felt a little stubble. Just a little.

He returned to the bench on the backside of the ruined cabin and sat on the plank to take inventory. The flash drive was safe in a pocket, as was the Hohner. His wallet was still there and he confirmed that it still contained $305. Everything else in the wallet was probably useless now. Using a credit card would be like shooting up a flare. But would he walk out from the trees to a time that even knew what a credit card was? It occurred to him that time itself had taken him off the grid of American commerce. He was a middle-class American consumer afloat at a time when hapless vagabond was more relevant.

A sound put him on alert. The soft slap of cloth or leather, then the rustling of people gathering themselves up. In the dark, just yards away, a group of heavily burdened folk emerged from the mist and underbrush. They threw sacks over their shoulders and donned hats. Men and women in well-worn homespun. And a few children.

All were black.

They stared at Harold and did not smile. In their eyes, suspicion.

Some kind of primitive racial divide, thought Harold.

So, it turned out, not all were black. A young white woman dressed in black with a hulking young black man at her hip emerged from the group to confront him. The woman came close enough to inspect Harold's face carefully.

"Thy name? Answer me!"

Harold looked into the face of a woman so determined and unavailing that he was temporarily unnerved over what might happen if he said the wrong thing.

"Harold," he said. "Harold Worthington."

She withdrew a few feet to take him in. A black bonnet tied around her throat hung behind her head, where an eruption of red hair was pinned here and there with combs. Her worn black dress covered her from neck to ankle, and Harold saw dandruff on her shoulders and some acne scars on her cheeks.

But the pale blue eyes caught his attention most. They sparked like steel on flint under bunched brows. Her hands were on her hips but were soon thrown up in exasperation.

"Why are these trials put in our path?" She turned to face her party, but clearly did not expect an answer. "Must servants of justice always encounter tribulation and uncertainty?"

She spun back to face Harold. "Interloper," she said. "At the very least, thou are an unwelcome interloper."

Impressions flashed through Harold's head. This could be a woman shouting while shoving a sign into the face of a cop. Or telling a reactionary professor his smug classroom perorations were tedious bullshit. Or staring daggers at a hostile crowd as she escorted a frightened woman into an abortion clinic.

She swept hair out of her face while regarding Harold as if he were a drunk who had fallen asleep on her doorstep. She heaved a deep breath and let it out in puffs until she needed to inhale again.

"What is thy purpose here?"

"I don't have a purpose here." Harold hoped this answer would satisfy her. He qualified this. "I'm here kind of by mistake. You see …"

She cut him off.

"Do thee have truck with slavers?"

Easy answer. "Slavers? No."

"Do thee live here?"

"No, I was injured down the road." Harold reached up to his head and realized no wounds remained. He stared into the distance. "Well, something strange is happening. I really don't belong here. You see…"

The woman's right hand came up and grasped his chin. Harold was speechless.

"My name is Elizabeth Baker and I am a Quaker. That's a plain truth." She pointed a finger at the imposing youth behind her. "And that is Amos."

Amos parted his lips in greeting, revealing a rack of teeth amid a bristling beard.

Elizabeth chewed her lower lip, as if weighing how much patience she should invest on this wastrel who could prove burdensome during her mission. She now braced Harold and gripped his suit lapels.

Harold realized his fate was in the hands of a woman who was, judging by the evidence so far, a drill sergeant of sorts.

Elizabeth sucked in her lips and popped them before she spoke. Her eyes never left Harold's face.

"Permit me to sum up plainly. There may be no harm in thee, but we cannot risk to leave thee behind. Thou are under the care of the Friends and now must accompany us. We are on a mission and you dare not interfere with it. You forsake your life if you do."

Harold stared blankly at the stranger. Was his life being threatened? He tilted his head as he tried to come up with an answer that would lower the temperature.

Elizabeth grabbed Harold's jaw again and pulled his face back to her.

"Is this understood?"

Harold could only nod.

Elizabeth turned to the youth next to her and Amos swung his tank turret of a head to face her.

"Amos. This man is now your charge."

Amos's gaze fixed on Harold, who he regarded like a burden that must be tolerated for now and attended to later. He threw a paw on Harold's shoulder to shove him forward. Almost instantly, Harold found himself trying to keep pace with this ragtag assembly, now on the march. A path lay before them, and they walked upon it to a destination Harold could not fathom.

He fell in step behind Elizabeth.

"Excuse me," he said. "But what year is this?"

She glanced at him in annoyance, then turned back to the path.

"Please. Indulge me."

She turned to smirk. "It is the year of our Lord 1851. That much is plain."

"Of course it is."

Harold's inattention to the path caused him to stumble.

"Yes. 1851." He rubbed his chin.

He looked back at the marchers. No further explanation was necessary, given the time and place. The place, in fact, had not changed. They were less than a day's walk north of the Mason-Dixon Line. The purpose of this procession was clear: escaped slaves, probably from Maryland or Virginia, were being led north to freedom by a band of Quakers.

Credit his American History teacher at Georgetown Prep.
He caught up again with Elizabeth.

"Where are we headed?"

Elizabeth arched her shoulders against her backpack.

"We will gather in Christiana in a few days. We have seasoned
Friends there. Then on to Philadelphia. It is my hope we can meet Mr.
Penn."

"Well, listen, I think this is a really noble cause. I have to con-
fess, however, that I am not of your time. That is to say …"

A gunshot rang out. The line of marchers froze.

"Slavers!" someone hissed.

It was like an order had been shouted. The group broke ranks
with discipline, leaving the path for shelter in the woods on either side.
Harold followed Elizabeth, Amos, and two others to a spot behind a
fallen maple. He lifted his head just above the tree trunk to see what
he could. A wall of deep forest darkness laughed back at him and a
loud voice broke the silence.

"Listen, you people there. Listen close to what I am about to
say. Your life may depend upon the next decision you make. We are
here to claim property belonging to owners according to the United
States of America and the Fugitive Slave Act."

After a pause, the voice took a coarser tone.

"No more parley. The niggers. Send them out."

Harold noticed that Amos, hunkered down next to him, now
wielded a revolver. Other slaves were also armed. It dawned on Harold
that a gunfight was highly probable and something seized up in his gut.
This nightmare was only getting worse.

Could you die more than a century before you were born?

"We are Quakers," Elizabeth shouted. "We shun violence and
abhor bloodshed. Nevertheless, we are caretakers of families. Those
families have men, those men are armed, and their weapons are aimed
at thee as we speak. I suggest you consider replacing thy arrogance with
forbearance, for thy own sake. No one need die here."

Good girl, thought Harold. Elizabeth was not finished.

"Thou may vouchsafe the law. But I say to thee now that this
fugitive slavery law is an obscenity and I will go to my death embattled
against it. Thou will get nothing from us. Return yourselves to Maryland with all thy God-hating immiseration. Thou are contemptible."

Harold looked at Elizabeth in a revelatory light. He never

imagined he would hear a woman of her stature face down a deadly
threat with an armload of invective.

Silence enfolded them now and Harold spoke to Elizabeth in
a low voice. He was afraid for her.

"Y'know, you Quakers, your embrace of pacifism may not fit
with certain realities in a situation like ..."

She turned a lifted eyebrow to him. *This? Now?*

A shotgun blast interrupted the thought and shredded leaves
in the trees overhead. More blasts erupted and the woods were filled
with the maddening racket of gunfire. Buckshot hit the fallen tree in
front of Harold and his face was raked with splinters. His gut was
about to give way as terror flushed through his bowels. This was not
his time! This was not his fight! He began to stand and raise his hands.

Suddenly, the front of his shirt was power lifted in the grip of
Amos. He could barely touch his toes to the ground.

"Y'all come with me."

Harold stumbled as Amos, who lifted Harold like an oversize
doll, force-marched him downhill. The forest floor was treacherous
footing, and Harold's knee hit a limestone berm. He was now too
numb with fear to care that he was probably bleeding. They plowed
through low branches of pines. Harold let go of any sense that he
ought to be in control. *We're leaving certain death,* he thought, *and being
dragged to certain death. Well, hell, here I go.*

A stream bed appeared in front of Harold and Amos, and suddenly it was no longer downhill. They splashed along the shallow, rock-
strewn trickle until another shot rang out and Amos let go a guttural
yell and collapsed with a splash into the stream. He clutched his left
leg. Even in the dark, Harold could see the rip in Amos' pants at the
back of his thigh, welling with blood.

Harold hovered, not sure how to help.

"Get going, man. I be fine." Amos held up his revolver and
waggled it. He gave Harold a broad wink.

Harold nodded, then bolted, trying to find footing in the shallow, rocky stream in the dark. His absurd shoes were not helping. He
was hardly fifty yards down the stream when a grinning, bearded, fat
man wearing a hat sporting a huge turkey feather bounded into his path
and planted both feet in the water. The man lifted his revolver. He was
chewing on something as he spoke. He also might have been drunk.
Harold couldn't take his eyes off the three-foot turkey feather. It

occurred to him that men with hat feathers could change them when they tired of the feather. The reverie soon evaporated.

The pursed lips under that feather said, "Going somewhere, nigger lover?" He lifted his hat. "Oh, no you doesn't."

He pointed and pulled the trigger.

Click.

This elicited a cluck of frustration from the rotund vigilante.

Harold, unarmed but adrenalized to the hilt, charged and spread out his arms, determined to wrap this son of a bitch around the waist and bring him down and pummel him. Harold could just feel the sweetness of his fists landing on this redneck peckerwood's face as he sprinted forward.

This peckerwood, however, held his pistol by the barrel and brought it down on Harold's head the moment Harold was at arm's length. The blow caught Harold in the center of the top of his head. The pain hardly registered as blackness enfolded him.

4

He awoke to the sound of gurgling water. It was the only sound. The dulcet patter of water coursing over rocks created a special harmony of pastoral repose. Or could have in other circumstances where the water didn't soak his shorts.

But what would his eyes behold? Harold opened them.

Daylight filled the stream bed. Unknowable insects heaved overhead in clouds. Harold's face rested on a flat rock. He was wet.

Again, he was wet.

Get out of the water.

Harold staggered to his feet and felt icy water draining through the crotch of his pants and down his legs.

Why?

He took inventory of the latest violations on his body by miscreants whose purpose had geographical, but not temporal, relevance to him. Time itself had condemned him to this place. This was a place from which to flee. Of this, he was certain.

Harold was also sure he was less than a mile from where he

abandoned the Porsche. *That happened more than a century, not ago but ahead,* he realized.

No coherence is attended to here that can reveal a pattern that is in any way discernable by science. The Mickey Mouse Club always had an "Anything Can Happen Day." But what about the next day? Ha.

He assessed his physical well-being and judged it frayed. Harold's suit had held together, but it was a soggy mess. He imagined there was grass in his hair, Then, he remembered he might have a head injury. He searched his head with his fingers. No wound. He slapped his wallet and checked pockets. Everything was in place. It was as if, he realized, his body had integrity, and so did the things he carried, and so did geography.

But time? Unstuck. A complete loss of integrity in that particular cosmic department. So where did that leave him?

Harold was wet and alone in the woods. That was bad enough. What was worse was that his future looked like the future of a cork in a flood. Was it his fate to bounce further into the past? Should he even care? Were there even rules here? If there were, what was the punishment for violating them?

Someone's got to know. I only need to find that person. Right? Yeah, someone knows.

He remembered an old remark by comedian Don Rickles: "Keep movin' so they don't throw dirt on ya."

Harold saw the end of the tree line and several buildings ahead. *Civilization. Yay. Maybe. Who knows? Probably wackdoodle like everything else so far. Let's see.*

In any case, he wasn't ready for the dirt. Not overhead.

Soon, no more trees. Harold emerged into clear-cut territory. There, fifty yards away, stood a motel with cabins that aligned in a crescent around a gravel driveway. In the center of the crescent, a rusted metal sign set in a concrete slab proclaimed this the Wayfarer Inn.

Harold recalled that the roadhouse he visited with Max and Benny had no vehicles prior to 1933. Here at the Wayfarer, he noticed, all the cars came off the line after 1963. Harold knew his Sixties iron. He spotted a couple of Mustangs and VW vans.

Modernity, of sorts. A recognizable cultural touchstone. Free at last—at least from the tyranny of trees and buckskin.

He strode confidently among the cabins, checking out the cars, pickups, and vans. Harold wanted to talk to the owners of each of these vintage rides. His American street legal mojo grew in anticipation as he walked to the motel office.

No effort had been made to make the office inviting. Even the welcome mat inside the door was torn. Harold brushed a rubber plant in the lobby, causing a big leaf to hit the floor. A cat darted away.

Professionalism in the hospitality industry had not yet reached this outpost.

Harold smiled. *I can deal with this.*

A teenager in a flannel shirt swept aside a curtain and took charge at the main desk. In one strange combination he blew out his chest and harrumphed. He knew he looked ridiculous, and Harold was in on the joke.

The clerk eyed the soggily draped figure before him. Brows knitted, he offered, "Can I help you?"

"I hope so. I could use some help."

Harold spotted a stack of magazines on a side table. The topmost featured Richard Nixon on the cover. He stifled a giggle. *Yup, figured with the cars in the lot.*

The teenaged giver-of-keys drew back into clerk mode at getting no response, donned a banal smile, as if to say, *Who was this drip who just walked in?*, and waited.

Harold put his hands down on the counter and gripped it with determination.

"I'll make this simple. I need a room for tonight and a way out of here in the morning."

"A way out? Something wrong with your car?"

"Listen, I'm not in the mood to do a lot of explaining. Suffice it to say I am currently without any form of transport. I kind of got … dropped off here."

The clerk, losing all interest, took a key from a slot and pushed it across the counter.

"You can have cabin eight. Thirty-seven dollars and twenty-six cents."

Harold pulled two twenties from his wallet and watched as the clerk rang him up with a literal dinging of the cash register and then handed back the change.

"Is there a bus that stops here?"

"Closest Greyhound or Trailways stop is in Chambersburg, about twenty-five miles from here on Lincoln Highway."

"How do I get to Chambersburg?"

The clerk shrugged. "Try your thumb. Works for a lot of people."

"Where am I exactly?"

"Breezewood. Bedford County, Pennsylvania."

"Never heard of it."

"Now you have."

Harold left the office, swinging the key by the wooden knob attached to it. The cars here, he now saw, were a mixed bag from the muscle car era, including two Mustangs, a Corvair, and a Ford Galaxy. Two Beetles, a Ford pickup, and a VW van rounded out the collection.

A bearded old man, wearing a stained Phillies baseball cap, slouched in a pitted steel armchair in front of his cabin and waved to Harold.

"Psst," he hissed, and crooked a finger. Harold walked over.

"Looking for a taste?" the coot asked through lips that might or might not be hiding teeth.

"I beg your pardon?"

"How about some shine?"

Harold was nonplussed, so the man lifted his skinny frame from the chair and, after scanning the horizon, put his mouth close to Harold's left ear.

"Made last Tuesday not two miles from here. Finest mash whiskey north of the Mason-Dixon Line."

Harold got it. "I gather you are talking about white lightning." Harold made a big show of organizing his thoughts as he rested chin on fist. "Hmm."

The fellow gripped Harold's arm, tilted his head, and drew Harold into his cabin. Inside, he dragged a box from under his bed. The box contained Mason jars filled with clear whiskey. He took one, unscrewed the cap, had a sip, and then offered it to Harold, who also had a sip and smacked his lips.

"I've had smoother. This won't make me go blind, will it?"

The coot bugged his rheumy eyes at Harold.

"I drink it."

"How much?"

"Five dollars."

Harold took a bill from his wallet and handed it over.

"You got a bag to put this in? I can't just walk around with this jar."

The man found Harold a paper bag and, in a moment, Harold was back outside. He took another pull on the corn in the jar, winced, then sucked in some air. *Something metallic in there, like BBs on the tongue.* As the heat from the alcohol rose to his face, Harold felt a bit of vigor return and he put a swagger in his step. *Hell, always face the killer with a martini in one hand and a woman's breast in the other.*

Music poured out of the VW bus, so Harold ambled over and noticed the rear door was partly open. He took another big pull, screwed the lid back on the jar, and raised two fingers in a peace sign.

"Dig it, man, outtasight!" he muttered to himself. He was about to give off a good vibe to his new freaky pals.

He bent at the waist to peer inside the van when, abruptly, he was shoved hard from behind and simultaneously grabbed by someone inside. Two seconds later, he was flopping on the floor of the van as the back door slammed shut. Strong hands pinned Harold down as a rag was stuffed in his mouth.

5

A week before Harold listened to the crows caw-
ing as he finished his sandwich on the side of the road, in a time when
time was still sane Harold sat in a Chinese restaurant sipping weak yellow tea and doing the crossword in the *Washington Post*. He was nervous
and obsessing over whether "peasant" was esne or peon.

An Asian man in a shiny gray suit, white shirt, and pink tie slid
into the booth across from Harold. He didn't remove his sunglasses.

Harold put his crossword aside and steepled his hands in anticipation. Harold had learned and practiced a formal Chinese welcome.

Before Harold could open his mouth, the man blurted in a
thick Chinese accent, "Show me something. Clock is running."

Harold exhaled.

"Well, you get right to the point, don't you? And do you mind
telling me your name?"

"Wong."

Harold pulled out his wallet, extracted his driver's license, and pushed it across the table.

"I am Harold Worthington, as you can see. This is my Maryland driver's license. Look at the address. Odenton. I have a condo there." He paused for effect. "That's next to Fort Meade, Maryland."

"You work for NSA."

"Not exactly. I work for a defense contractor. Our contract is with the NSA and other agencies in the intelligence alphabet soup."

Harold leaned in and lowered his voice.

"What I am about to tell you …"

"No fuck around."

"Excuse me?" Harold said.

"Don't tell. Show. No fuck around."

The man slapped the table, startling Harold, who recovered with a chuckle. Nodding, he reached into an accordion file next to him in the booth, withdrew a single sheet of paper, and pushed it across to Wong. Wong regarded it with mild disdain and did not pick it up.

"Perhaps I should explain what it is you are looking at."

Wong crossed his arms and noisily sucked his teeth.

Sheesh, Harold thought.

"It's a page from the minutes of a meeting in the Kremlin. You heard that correctly. The Kremlin. It's *eyes only*, et cetera, et cetera. You might wonder how it came to be that I am showing you this at a restaurant here in Silver Spring."

Harold waited for acknowledgement he never received. Wong was Buddha, Harold guessed, deep into his path and barely tolerating the presence of a hopeless outlier. Harold sighed again.

"The reason is because of a computer worm designed in Langley that opened a back door in Moscow. It's a beaut. Makes the Morris worm look like a Model T. We're talking about a cyber architecture so advanced …"

Wong began combing his hair with his fingers while suppressing a yawn.

Harold rolled his head backward and looked at the red-painted restaurant ceiling with little dragons. *Why did this Chinese national pick this ersatz Moo Goo joint in the D.C. suburbs to meet?*

"Anyway, it came across my desk because my new job is looking at data from Russians with top clearances."

"And this is important to the People's Republic because …"

This is more like it, Harold thought. *Horse trading has begun.*

"The Russians will pay for it. They will trade for it. Not only do they learn about an opening in their back door and close it, but it's leverage. You know how it works. Governments always want stuff that can embarrass another government. Intelligence, let's face it, is a commodity that should be listed on Wall Street's big board."

Wong removed his sunglasses and started to polish them, eyes cast down. "Value is obscure."

Harold could almost feel the hook set.

"It's once in a lifetime, my friend." Harold laced his hands behind his head and arched his back. "You will not see the likes of me again, I guarantee." *Easy. Don't oversell.*

Now it was Harold's turn to sit mute.

"I repeat, why bring this to People's Republic?"

Harold made a *tsk-tsk* sound. He wanted Wong to see him thinking. How to explain such a complicated subject? He leaned forward and made a cards-on-the-table gesture.

"I don't want to deal with the Russians. Too many ... wheels inside wheels. I sell it to you, you sell it to them. Or the Israelis. Or the Iranians. I don't care. It's all on a flash drive. You want to know what the Russian brass is up to? Even if you don't, someone else does. I guarantee you, someone wants this."

"And you have this zip file now?"

"Like in my pocket? Hell, no. Let's just say I know its whereabouts. It is in my control."

Harold watched as Wong lifted the sheet of paper, scanned it briefly, then folded it once, twice, three times, and tucked it into his inside jacket pocket.

"We want to see more," Wong said.

Harold nodded in sage understanding.

"That can be done. Meanwhile, let's talk turkey. You understand turkey?"

"Some poultry."

"Sold by the pound."

Harold poured himself and Wong a bit of urine-colored tea, then had another thought.

"Want a real drink?"

Wong gave nothing away, but said, "Buffalo Trace."

"Bourbon man!" Harold said with new respect. "Me too." He signaled for the waiter.

6

Strong hands still pinned Harold down in the back of the hippie van. He was choking on the rag and squirmed helplessly.

The male voice close to his ear was quiet and disciplined.

"Any scream or struggle and you get this or this." A baseball bat was waved in front of Harold's eyes. It was withdrawn and replaced with a revolver.

"Understood?"

Harold nodded.

The hands released Harold, and the rag was yanked roughly from his mouth. Harold slowly drew himself to a sitting position, smacking his lips, and assessed the situation. Before Harold in this freak folk capsule were three of them: a white man and a black man in the back of the van with him, and a woman in the driver's seat. Three sets of eyes strafed Harold with undisguised suspicion.

The white man, with a weedy pile of dark blonde hair and a five-day beard, wore a fatigue jacket and jeans. He gave the bat a slow twirl and moved his jaw from side to side as he regarded Harold.

"You got about ten seconds to explain yourself, mister."

A spark of corn whiskey bravery emerged.

"I don't have to tell you …"

Fatigue Jacket dropped the bat and picked up the revolver.

Harold examined the other faces and saw no sympathy.

He smiled, recalling Vince Guaraldi's "Cast Your Fate to the Wind." *What the hell.*

"Well, you see, I'm from the future. I'm a spy agency contractor who is now a fugitive from government agents. I stole sensitive secrets and I was planning to sell them to China. Then, I was betrayed to the FBI. I bolted, but my car broke down a mile from here. Some bootleggers, slaves, and Quakers gave me a hand. I walked through the woods and here I am."

The pronouncement hung in the air like a pinata for long seconds before full-throated laughter erupted. Even Harold joined in.

The tension evaporated. The laughter gave way to snorts and giggles, and Harold wiped his eyes with a sleeve.

Fatigue Jacket kicked in, "Well, all I have to say is, far-fucking out. You have my blessing. That's some trip you're on."

More laughter. A sense of shared mischief prevailed.

"So, hippies with guns?" Harold dared the question. "Is this what it's come to?"

The man hefted his bat again and cleared his throat.

"I ain't no hippie. I am former staff sergeant Daniel Bodine, United States Army. I am currently en route, as we say. This here is Jamal."

Jamal had been watching quietly and, at this reference, raised an eyebrow.

Daniel continued. "Jamal has been drafted, but he's not going to serve. We are taking him to Toronto."

The woman in the driver's seat took the floor.

"I have this sister in Toronto, dig? So that's where we are going to give Jamal asylum. You understand asylum? It's medieval. The monks used to have these arches as you entered the monastery. Past the arch, free and clear. Even the king couldn't touch you." She paused. "By the way, I'm Tanya."

Tanya shook Harold's hand. Her narrow face was framed by two pencil-thin braids. She wore a peasant blouse over her wiry frame and a snake bracelet over her bicep. Harold would bet she was a Janis

Joplin fan.

Harold played his ace. "Got room for a passenger?"

Jamal piped up now. "You know the drill. Gas, grass, or ass."

Harold retrieved his wallet and riffled through the bills for the trio to see. Smiles all around.

Harold found a couple pillows and got comfortable. "What music you got?"

"How about Quicksilver," Daniel offered.

"'Who Do You Love?' Yeah," Harold replied. His parents used to play this. They even danced in the living room to it.

Daniel lit a joint as Quicksilver Messenger Service redeveloped the old Bo Diddley tune and the jet-propelled guitars swung in.

Harold took a toke on the joint and looked at a poster taped to the inside wall of the van with the message "Today is the first day of the rest of your life."

He started laughing again as he passed the joint and wondered what time it was. A few more tokes and he didn't care.

7

Back in his cabin at the Wayfarer, the receding buzz from the VW van still goosing his mojo, Harold lay on his bed, singing the refrain, "Have another hit!" The double shot of shine and vitamin J was wearing off when he heard a knock at the door.

"I don't need housekeeping. Come back later," he shouted.

A man's voice answered. "Someone's here to see you."

"Who?"

"Can't talk out here. You understand."

Harold walked to the window and tried to see who was out there. Bad angle, couldn't see. He considered, then went to the door and attached the chain before opening. He peered out through the crack.

"Please tell me …" was all he got out before a tremendous kick blasted the door open, ripping the chain from the wall.

Harold staggered backwards as a man in a trench coat barreled in and shoved Harold onto the bed. The man grabbed Harold by the lapels, lifted him to his feet, and quickly frisked him from armpits to

ankles. The assailant shoved Harold back onto the bed and comman-
deered the sole armchair, which he settled into.

"Just cool your heels a while, pal. You got visitors," he said.
He pulled out rolling papers and a drawstring bag of tobacco and began to roll a cigarette.

It was quiet for a moment until the door opened fully and a
couple in their sixties dressed in top-dollar country comfort entered
and took a look around. They were absurdly examining a photo of the
Bridge of Sighs in Venice on the wall when the woman turned around
to face Harold. Then the man also turned around.

Harold was slack jawed. He expected surprises, but not this.
"Mom. Dad."

His mother, Helen, was first to speak.

"Honey, are you okay?"

Harold could only utter, "How did you find me?"

Helen gestured to the man in the armchair.

"Dash here is an excellent detective. He's a Pinkerton."

Dash nodded cheerfully as he tongued his roll-up.

Harold's father, Jack, strode forward.

"Harold, the FBI have been to see us. It was a Mr. Wu. You
may know him as a Chinese spy called Wong. In fact," his father came
closer and tilted his head to the side, "he's a Princeton graduate and a
special agent for the FBI. He has a thirty-five-foot sloop in Annapolis
and season tickets to the Redskins. Jesus Christ."

His father sighed and lifted his hands.

"Have you no radar for the heat? My God."

His mother picked it up.

"It's something about stolen classified documents. Darling,
what have you done now?"

Parental eyes regarded Harold with pity and awaited an answer.
Harold gathered his defense. "I'm, uh, a whistleblower, like
Snowden."

His father and mother exchanged glances. Time for his father
to weigh in again.

"Aha. Like Snowden. Of course. He acted to protect American
privacy," Jack said, then tilted his head. "You're peddling secrets for
money. Of course. I see. Of course."

Harold, stung, shook his head. Maybe he could make sense of
this.

"We are talking about underhanded stuff. Computer worms and covert security breaches. And ..."

"Honey," his mother interrupted, "listen to me. It's all spy versus spy. It has gone on for centuries. It's how governments play games with each other. It has nothing to do with you and me or any regular American. It's just games. But if you trick the dice, they make you pay. You have tricked the dice."

Suddenly, Dash was out of his chair and at the door. Daniel and Jamal were outside looking in.

Daniel spotted Harold and leaned insolently against the door frame. "Hey, man, is everything cool?" He inspected his fingernails.

Jack Worthington clasped his hands behind his back, rocking at the waist, and made a show of examining the button on Daniel's fatigue jacket. The button said "sds" in red on a white background. The riser on the d ended in a fist.

Jack said, "'If we appear to seek the unattainable ...'"

Daniel rocked his jaw with his hand and took a new look at Jack.

"'We do so to avoid the unimaginable.' You know the Port Huron Statement?"

They regarded each other in silence until Jack broke it.

"Worker Student Alliance?"

"Those Maoist cocksuckers? Progressive Labor can kiss my wobbly ass. I'm Revolutionary Union."

"Buncha bourgeois adventurists. Reformist lackeys expiating white guilt."

Jack, enjoying the moment, raised his hand for a high five, lowered it when none came. Daniel crossed his arms across his barrel chest and tilted his head, awaiting more.

"Well," Jack said. "I was Revolutionary Youth Movement, but I bailed when Rudd and Ayers and those Weather assholes took over in Chicago. Kinda dug Bernadine, though." He gazed over to his wife. "Then I met Harold's mother in Vermont."

Helen became animated.

"We had a cheese collective outside Brattleboro. Still do. We were the Hairy Dairy for a while, but the focus groups nixed that. Now, we're the Sunshine Meadowlark Dairy Collective."

Helen's pride in capitalist achievement gave her pause, but she plunged ahead. In for a penny, in for a big pitch.

"We ship to all fifty states. We do maple syrup, too. Check out our website," she said. "We were even on *Oprah*."

Jack said, "Cabot wanted to take us over. We said …"

Jack and Helen spoke in unison: "Big cheese, go fuck yourself!"

They fell into a giggling fit. Daniel, Jamal, Harold, and Dash were nonplussed.

Jack coughed into his fist.

"Anyway, Harold, your mom and I won't betray you, but we suggest you turn yourself in. What you have done so far amounts to a security breach, not treason. At least that's what Wu said. He probably can't be trusted, but there you are."

Jack took out his wallet and extracted a card, which he handed to Harold.

"This is our friend, Rudy. You remember him from the lake house in Northeast Kingdom? The movement lawyer who had that nudist girlfriend? He's waiting to hear from you and can arrange bail."

Jack perused the faces in the doorway.

"You seem to have made friends. All of you are welcome to our cabin in Northeast Kingdom."

With that, Jack, Helen, and Dash departed. Dash tipped his fedora as he flipped his spent roll-up into the parking lot.

Daniel took the lawyer's card from Harold's hand and tore it up.

"C'mon, we gotta head north. You coming?"

Harold whooshed out some air and tried to shut down the cacophony in his head. So many choices swirling overhead. So many directions to follow. So many.

"Sure."

In the parking lot, Daniel hauled a duffel from his cabin and tossed it into the back of the VW van. Tanya took the wheel and turned the key in the ignition as the others climbed in the back.

Just as Tanya got it in gear and they pulled out, a beige sedan careened crazily into the lot, raising dust, until it scraped to a halt directly behind them. The sedan's doors flew open and out sprung two soldiers in helmets with hands on gun holsters.

"Who's that?" asked Tanya, gazing in her rearview.

Daniel could see them now. Ice filled his veins.

"It's Mary Fucking Poppins! MPs! Vamoose!"

Daniel bolted to the shotgun seat, slammed open the glove

compartment, and pulled out a Smith & Wesson Model 60. He checked the cylinder. Fully loaded.

Tanya caught Daniel's eye, covering her mouth with her hand. "Don't," she pleaded.

Stone-faced, Daniel lifted his finger, pointed it at her, then at the road ahead. She accelerated.

The van sprayed gravel as it lurched out of the parking lot onto Lincoln Highway, gaining speed in sparse traffic. But the sedan, in pursuit, was overtaking. It pulled alongside on the left and the MP on the passenger side had a shotgun resting on his forearm out the window. He smiled at Tanya and winked. She hit the gas and the van surged ahead. As Tanya slammed the accelerator to the floor, the van seemed to lift vertically as it blasted forward.

The MP in pursuit lowered the shotgun's aim to the left rear tire of the van.

But before he could fire, the van's rear door flew open with a bang, and there was Daniel, lying on his stomach, elbows draping over the rear bed of the van. Jamal gripped his ankles to keep Daniel stationary. Daniel held the revolver in both hands. He fired.

The sedan's exterior rear-view mirror shattered, spraying glass into the MP's face. The MP fired the shotgun wildly as he pulled back into the car. The driver threw the wheel to the left and the sedan shot sideways. Its tires wailed as it turned its right side to oncoming traffic.

Tanya tried to get past the sedan, but a truck bore down in the opposite direction. The semi's horn ripped the air like the screech of an animal being eaten as it braked, the trailer slewing to the left like a door slowly closing, shutting in the face of the oncoming sedan and van.

Harold, staring out the windshield, was transfixed as he saw the view completely obscured by the onrushing semi.

Tanya was now standing on the brake, her butt lifted off the seat and her back arched as she stiff-armed the steering wheel. One side of her mouth was yanked down to her chin and her eyes bugged with fear.

A thunderous orgy of caving sheet metal and flying glass erupted.

Harold, lifted into the air, thudded into the back of the driver's seat toward the van's open doors, and was tossed onto the roadway. He rolled, then found himself at rest, lying on the asphalt on his back.

Harold knew he was bleeding, and he heard the glass shards sliding off his face as they clinked onto the roadway. He heaved a sigh and shut his eyes.

Who could say how much time had passed? Time now was a roulette wheel that spun steadily until the marble grabbed a slot and the whole thing slowed down to reveal a location with a number attached. It was a location in time, not space. The space had yet to change. ✹ (MITCHNER !)

Harold opened his eyes. He was still on his back, but in the woods. Above his face, leaves. Lots of leaves. He was lying in a bevy of shrubbery. He heard a slow clopping sound and raised himself to a sitting position.

The clopping sound was horses' hooves and he was looking at the legs of two horses. His gaze lifted and he saw two Indians astride their mounts. They were Senecas in traditional buckskin, beads, and feathers.

The two young warriors regarded Harold solemnly for a while, judged him unworthy of their attention, and continued onward on their mounts. White man lying on the ground under a bush? No percentage in further investigation.

Harold touched his face and hair. No damage. He stood. It was turning dark and his ears picked up a sound not too distant. Now he could see a campfire. He headed in that direction with an inkling of what he would find.

The strains of a rhythmic chant grew louder as Harold walked across the ragged forest floor. He reached a small clearing. Before him, a small crowd gathered around a snapping fire and sang. They were wrapped in blankets, and the lambent firelight fitfully illuminated their African faces. They clapped as they sang.

"Be so glad," a voice intoned.

"When the sun go down," was the response.

"I wanna sleep."

"When the sun go down."

"Lie down."

"I wanna lie down."

"Lie down."

"I wanna lie down."

Several faces turned as Harold entered the circle. He found a place to sit. Introductions were no longer necessary. He pulled out his harmonica and blew some riffs to accompany the songs. His harmony merged with theirs. The fire snapped and sent up sparks, then resumed its soft glow.

He felt someone arrive at his side.

"The slaver struck thee, but I see no injury now," Elizabeth said.

She gently took Harold's jaw in her hand to rotate his head to her. For Harold, there was something electric in it. No woman had ever treated his face this way.

Harold smiled, still looking at the fire. Elizabeth's stern voice from before had yielded to something more companionable.

"That was a long time ago," Harold said. "How is Amos?"

"He can walk. He has many scars. One more matters little."

Harold nodded. He and Elizabeth exchanged a look. Then, they turned their gaze back to the fire.

Elizabeth gazed at an approaching figure and said, "There's someone among us thee should meet."

It was a weathered black woman of indeterminate age with a scarf tied over her head and a shawl over her shoulders. Her face was coarsely featured, etched by a history of onslaught and survival.

Elizabeth said, "This is our conductor, Harriet Tubman. We call her Moses."

Harriet did not look at Harold but had a slight smile on her face. "Nice fire tonight."

As Harriet arranged her shawl, Harold saw she was armed with a small pistol.

"Shot any slavers lately?"

Harriet smiled again, but held her gaze on the fire.

"Ain't just slavers. I'll shoot a slave he make trouble during a foray. Be free or be dead."

"No wonder you have a reputation."

"I have a dis-reputation."

"How many slaves have you brought out?"

Harriet adjusted her shawl and sighed. "Could be hundreds. Could be more. Can't really say. Could have been thousands, but some people don't know they're slaves."

She turned to look at Harold, her face a personal challenge.

Now, it was Harold staring at the fire. A new conversational direction emerged.

"You must have serious enemies."

Harriet, nodding, considered this.

"On this day, yes I do. But this day will pass. A new day is coming. That's what God tells me."

Harriet rose and patted Harold's shoulder as she left. The fire was dying and the group was bedding down. Harold propped his back against a tree and gave in to the weight of fatigue.

"Holy Mary, mother of God, pray for us sinners now and at the hour of our death. Amen."

The words comforted Harold and he fell into sleep.

9

Harold awoke, knees drawn up, leaning side-
ways into a tree. He was alone, as he expected. He brushed leaves from
his lap and pulled himself to his feet. He stretched his neck as he began
to walk. After about ten minutes, another noise joined the forest am-
biance of birds and wind-rustled trees.

Traffic.

Harold tilted his head and strained to hear.

Yes, traffic. No question.

A tree line came into view and he headed for it as the thrum
and snore of cars and trucks grew in volume. Now, he saw a clearing
stretching beyond the tree line. His pace picked up as Harold realized
that his destination now might his own, familiar time period.

The clearing was a meadow on a downhill slope. Harold
worked his way down in the morning sunshine through overgrown
grass. Raptly, he gazed ahead. At the bottom of the slope, the grass
turned to asphalt and the ground leveled out at a sprawling parking lot
that encompassed a cluster of gas stations, restaurants, and motels.

Bob Evans, Denny's, McDonald's all looked perky beneath towering signs. The inns included Holiday, Quality, Days, and Budget.

This is more like it!

He headed toward a building with a massive sign on the roof that simply said Gateway. Smaller signs offered a video arcade, pizza, gift shop, and oven-fresh bakery. The glass doors opened to air-conditioned comfort and a sign that said, "Welcome to Breezewood, the Town of Motels." Meandering around the lobby were the traveling denizens of America, some them still semi-hypnotized from the road. If they had any kind of short-term need that would require professional attention—whether body, mind, or internal combustion engine—this was the place.

The gift shop had a book and map section labeled "Local Interest." He pulled down a book entitled *Breezewood: An American Crossroads for Centuries*. Leafing through it, he saw antique photos and engravings—Civil War soldiers, pioneers in covered wagons, Revolutionary War soldiers, Victorian coaches, Indians on horseback.

And here was a picture of Harriet Tubman. The scarf on her head was the one she wore at fireside the previous night.

Surrounding Harold was an array of revolving kiosks bearing sunglasses, teddy bears, folding knives, individualized keychains arranged in alphabetical order, shot glasses with the catchy "Breezewood: Town of Motels" tagline. Harold tried on a pair of sunglasses and looked into the little mirror on the kiosk. He had twigs in his hair. He re-racked the sunglasses and went to find the men's room.

The men's room was a huge walk-in space with enough urinals to line a bowling alley lane. Low murmurs prevailed, flushing sounds and the occasional piping up of a little boy could be heard. He took his measure in the mirror above the sink. He turned on the hot water, squirted some soap from a dispenser, and began washing his hands. A man came up beside him, placed a Dopp kit on the counter, zipped it open, and retrieved something. Then he stepped into an empty toilet stall.

With some circumspection, Harold peered into the open kit.

A cellphone.

Five seconds later, Harold was out the bathroom door with the cell in his pocket.

In the restaurant, Harold slid into a booth. A waitress immediately dropped off utensils wrapped in a napkin bound in a paper ring.

She placed a glass of water on the table and handed Harold a menu.

Harold took a deep breath and dialed the cell. After a few rings, his eyes lit up.

"Hi, Melanie. Is Amber there?"

He scanned the room for anyone who might be on the hunt for a cellphone thief. No one was paying attention.

"Amber! It's Harold! Yeah. Uh huh. Well, the reason I'm calling is that I need a big favor. Yes I do, indeed. I need a ride. I'm stuck somewhere without a car. It's a long story, but I wondered if you could pick me up."

Harold raked his lower teeth across his upper lip and looked upward in supplication.

"I'm in Breezewood. Yeah, it's in Pennsylvania. It's just off I-70 and the Pennsylvania Turnpike. Yeah, crazy, I know."

As he listened, confidence drained from his face.

"Amber, it'll take you two hours, tops. You just take 270 up to 70 and shoot west. Amber, I wouldn't ask if there was some other way. C'mon, I deserve a break today."

His face brightened. His eyes closed, and he jiggled a knee in happiness.

"Lover, that's terrific. You are the ace in my deck. The cream in my coffee. We'll have a nice time together riding back. Meet me at the Gateway Travel Plaza. You can't miss it."

"Someone wants to speak with me?" Harold's face clouded "Who?"

Harold's mouth was working now and his eyes cast about in panic as he listened to the male voice on the other end of the call.

"Listen, Mr. Wong, or Mr. Wu, or whoever the fuck you are, you can try and find me but I am out of your reach. Listen, I told Amber I was in Breezewood, but I could really be anywhere."

Now, his breathing was shallow and his eyes wouldn't focus. His gripped the phone tightly.

"We can work something out? Is that what you're asking? Yeah, in Leavenworth."

Harold shook his head as the tip of his tongue worried a molar.

"Try me, motherfucker. Just try me. Any time. Any time. Any fucking time!"

He cut the connection, lowered his right elbow to the table, and pressed his forehead into the heel of his right hand. His chest heaved.

"You okay, hon?" It was the waitress.

One last heave, then he managed a smile. "Uh, make it a coffee to go and a bagel with cream cheese, also to go."

After the waitress left, Harold drank his water and took stock.

Wu knew where he was, but Harold figured he had time. There seemed to be options of escape that were not geographic, after all. Just head for the tree line.

The waitress brought his coffee and bagel in a sack and he gave her a few bills, noting that the contents of his wallet were shrinking.

He slid out of the booth and ambled toward the glass doors when he saw two men slouched at a corner table, one of them picking his teeth and the other reading a newspaper.

Harold froze.

He rotated in their direction and took careful note of the two familiar faces.

Max and Benny, the bootleggers. Now, however, they were not in bowler hats and braces. Max wore a leather vest over a rock band T-shirt. Harold could tell by the armpit bulge he had something holstered under there. Benny was clothed in Armani, with an open-at-the-throat lavender silk shirt. Both wore sunglasses. Both basked in an air of insouciance.

Harold stared. They noticed his attention and their brows knitted as they took him in.

"Max and Benny."

Max, still with the toothpick, looked out the window before turning his gaze back toward Harold. "Do we know you?"

Harold hesitated. But, in for a penny, in for a pound. *Or a fifth. Or a kilo.*

"I was out cold on the highway. You stopped your truck and picked me up. We made a delivery to a speakeasy. Mamie's."

Benny reached up and, with infinite deliberation, gathered the front of Harold's shirt in his fist and pulled him down to take a closer look. Benny bared his teeth and tilted his head to check Harold's profile.

Then, making a sharp sucking sound through his right canine, Benny released Harold and gave him a pat on the cheek and a smile.

"You're the ragamuffin. You blew harp with Robert."

"Wow, you remember. Wow. Seems like a long time ago."

Benny shrugged. "Not really."

"So, what are you guys up to now."

"Business."

Benny arched his back and his jacket came open. A nine milli-meter caused the bulge.

"But Prohibition is over. Booze is legal now. How can you have customers …."

Max, grinning, held up a hand. He tipped his head to the win-dow. Harold swiveled to look out at the parking lot.

He had to laugh. Of course.

A rock band caravan consumed the rear part of the parking lot. Two semis and a bus covered entirely with images, including the fierce eyes of a black man staring out at you. Stylized lettering read "Bleed You Dry. Get sucked out by the master, Rajah XXX."

As Harold took this in, he realized the entourage from the car-avan was entering the restaurant. The roadies, it seemed, were first. One reached into his pants to scratch his balls. Then he sniffed his fingers in curiosity. Another dropped a lit cigarette into a planter.

Then came the groupies, with strategically torn gaping holes in their clothes, melting mascara, and neon-streaked lawnmower-styled hair. Their lipstick looked as though it had been applied with a kitchen sponge. One groupie flexed her bicep to pop out a tattoo for her friend's amusement.

Arriving last were two others. Harold was transfixed.

The first was Robert Johnson, but not the Smithsonian Collec-tion blues singer now. He wore solid white—a hoodie, jeans, sneakers. He had removed his shades and walked straight ahead, his gaze fixed on no one and nothing. These were the eyes. These were the eyes on the side of the bus.

By his side was a woman who spoke on a cellphone. She wore low-rise jeans that gave a flash of navel, and a leather jacket over a T-shirt with something written in Japanese. Her red hair was in a shag.

Harold recognized the woman as Quaker abolitionist Elizabeth Baker.

Elizabeth examined a clipboard as she walked and talked on her cellphone.

"Yeah, we're stopped for lunch. We just left Clair Brothers in Lititz. No, it's not Bruce's leftovers. I know sound equipment. Give me some credit."

Meanwhile, the entourage had spotted Max and Benny. It was old home week.

A roadie walked up and gripped the front of his own shirt like a hopeless tubercular in extremis.

"Faddah, I got dis pain. It's awful, dis pain I got. Won't ya help another Catholik. I was a altah boy, faddah. I need relief."

Another stretched out his arms, tilted his head, unfocused his eyes, and staggered.

"Brains," he moaned. "I want to eat brains."

Max and Benny winked and smiled at them indulgently. These were the preliminaries. Deals would come later.

Elizabeth, barely concealing her annoyance, called out, "Everyone gets a hamburger, fries, and Coke. We have a half hour."

"Cheeseburger!" piped up another.

She turned to the waitress. "I'll have a Cobb salad. Robert?"

Robert, without looking up from his phone, said, "Glass of water. Six ice cubes."

Harold was at their booth, standing and waiting for his moment.

Elizabeth finally looked up. "Yes?"

"I, uh, can see you're busy, but I have a question. Well, not really a question. See, I think we've met before."

"No autographs," said Robert, still absorbed by his phone.

Harold plowed forward.

"Robert, you were performing 'Crossroad Blues' and I was at the bar with my little Hohner and blew a minor accompaniment. It was in the joint on the Lincoln Highway, I think."

Harold reached into his pocket, pulled out the harmonica, and gave it a little flourish.

With the alacrity of a bored sloth, Robert lifted his eyes and scrutinized Harold.

"When was that, exactly?"

"You don't remember?"

"I been to a lot of places, met a lot of people. Might have met you. Might not."

"It was right here."

Johnson nodded and offered a smile. He began cleaning his shades with a cloth.

"That could be, my friend. That could be."

Harold turned to Elizabeth, who had been listening with mild interest.

"Elizabeth, the last time I saw you …" He gazed out to the tree line, then back at her.

"That was a long time ago," she replied.

Harold recognized her crooked grin and his heart thudded. She still radiated impatience. Hell, she was still the boss.

"Naw. Not really. It was practically yesterday," Harold said.

Elizabeth placed her cell on the table, rested her back against the padded booth, folded her arms, and took a long appraising look at Harold. He flushed, pinned like an insect by her gaze.

Outside, brakes chirped and tires scraped as two big sedans and a Chevy Surburban skidded to rest in the parking lot. Doors blew open, revealing men in suits.

Agents fanned out into the restaurant, pressing fingers into earbuds, eyes strafing the customers.

"Whoo-hoo, motherfucker! The Feds are here to save us!" It was one of the roadies.

A groupie piped up. "Why'rnt you out shooting black folks? Ain't that your job?" She high fived her friend.

An agent built like a beer truck lifted cell to ear.

"Wu? Still looking."

A white guy in sunglasses sat in a booth wearing an ivory hoodie pulled up over his head. Robert and Elizabeth avoided looking at the target beside them. The hooded white guy studied the menu assiduously as the agents fanned out.

"Let's get on the bus," Robert said.

"I'm going to finish my salad." Elizabeth smiled.

This woman will never be stampeded, Harold thought. *Or stop giving orders. Or stop holding men by the jaw.*

The musicians and entourage, some still carrying their hamburgers, filed into the bus and took their usual places. Some donned headphones, a few pulled out Japanese comic books. Others checked their phones.

Robert gestured for Harold to follow him, and both boarded the bus and the narrow aisle to the back where Robert parted a curtain and ushered him in. Harold lifted a stack of magazines to make a place to sit. Robert's photo was on the cover of every magazine. One headline read, "Robert: Whatever it Takes, Goddamn You."

Harold sat and gazed out the window to his left. A convoy of World War II vehicles passed by.

Robert picked up a guitar and started bending notes with a tender abrasion. Harold, rapt, could hear a thread in the mournful tones that stretched back to that roadhouse in 1933. Robert had a talent that was some kind of alchemy, an ability to reach out into nothingness, close the fist, then open it to reveal something both unexpected and precisely appropriate.

Harold broke the silence. "Where are you going?"

"When?"

"Now."

"We got Consol Energy tonight in Pittsburgh, then on to Chicago."

Robert took out a bottle and poured two shots. They clinked glass and tossed back.

"Tequila?" Harold asked.

"Sotol. It's from Chihuahua. Smoother. Hard to find in the states, but I get it from Max and Benny."

Robert poured two more and set his guitar aside.

"I don't know what I'm supposed to do." Harold tossed off the shot.

"Put one foot in front of the other. Stay on top of the grass. That's one plan."

Harold laughed. "And don't get dirt thrown on ya." He paused, and then asked, "And go where?"

"Depends where you are."

"I know where I am. I don't know *when* I am."

"Ain't time a bitch?" Robert said.

The curtain parted and Elizabeth entered. Robert offered her the bottle, but she demurred.

"You know I don't drink."

"Against y'alls religion."

"Something like that."

Elizabeth was just getting comfortable when the bus driver poked his head through the curtain. "Head count checks. ETD?"

Elizabeth checked her phone, flashed ten fingers. The driver left. Harold lifted a finger for attention.

"Y'know, maybe I could help out on this tour."

He pulled out his harmonica and honked a note or three. He

tilted his head.

Robert and Elizabeth looked at each other. Elizabeth then turned to Harold.

"This is not your mission."

"Well, how about just a ride to Pittsburgh?"

10

The tour bus door thunked open and out stepped Harold. He stood in the parking lot, watching as the bus grunted to life and, with a squeal, started to roll. As the bus passed, and the rest of the convoy geared up, a rear curtain rustled, then slowly opened. Elizabeth smiled weakly, leaning her forehead into the glass. She pressed her palm to the window as the bus pushed onward. Harold would always remember that image.

Harold slogged back to the Gateway Travel Plaza. The Feds and their vehicles were gone. Benny and Max were gone. It was hardly mid-afternoon and the sun hung listlessly. Half the day stretched ahead, more than he thought he could endure in this massive waystation that offered food, gas, bedding, and a toilet in safe, sanitary surroundings to thousands on their way to some place that mattered to them.

Too much to endure for one left behind. *Fuck 'em.* Harold eyed the tree line.

Ahead, just downhill from the interstate, Harold arrived at a flea market. Rows of folding tables, some set under canvas cover, lined the rear of the Gateway parking lot. The tables offered the expected baby clothes, knick-knacks, flatware, clock radios, flower vases, and ceramics. Harold joined the browser crowd.

He found a harmonica in a case. Harmonicas are micro-engineering masterpieces and this was a possible treasure, a Hohner Triumph, still in its distinctive red box. He opened the box and examined the instrument for rust and wear. It was in pristine condition. Harold's heart raced. In the marketplace, it was money in the bank. He had to laugh. *That idiot Stanislaus is still trying to peddle a Hohner Meisterklasse that was supposedly stolen from Bob Dylan's dressing room at the hungry I in San Francisco. Hah, as if. The hungry i had no dressing room, and Dylan would never be that neglectful. What a fool was Stanislaus,* Harold thought.

"Uh, how much for this old harmonica?"

A big-boned woman cut short her conversation with another big-boned woman and sauntered over. Harold held it up casually, meanwhile inspecting a set of steak knives.

"That'll cost you twenty bucks."

Harold pretended to be enthralled with the steak knives.

"Fifteen."

"I don't want to horse around. Twenty." It wasn't that warm, but she pulled out a handkerchief and wiped the back of her neck. Then, she blew her nose into the rag.

Harold sighed, opened his wallet wearily, and handed over a bill.

She took it and Harold, poker face intact, pocketed the instrument, which he knew was worth four hundred. But it might go into his collection. He had to laugh. *Collection? When will I see that again?*

As he scanned the tree line, Harold noticed that the two big-boned women were looking up at the highway, as were others.

Harold looked, too, eyes wide.

11

On the highway, a company of British colonial soldiers approached. Harold instantly recognized them as portrayed in history books and movies about the French and Indian War, and the American Revolution. The Redcoats marched in ragged order along the highway with a few horse-drawn wagons rolling behind an officer on horseback. They were a pin on the war map of General William Howe, part of a maneuver to encircle forces of the Continental Congress.

Motorists in cars and trucks used the berm to circumvent the brigade. Several honked, either in support of, or annoyed by, the display.

The officer on horseback who led the group raised a hand and shouted something inaudible. His men halted and began finding places to sit. A convenience store occupied the opposite side of the highway, advertising coffee and a doughnut for two dollars. Harold watched as several of the soldiers wandered in that direction.

Business resumed at the flea market. Harold heard a woman

squeal, "Oh my God, is this carnival glass?" A little girl, tugging at her mother's skirt, complained, "I'm hungry. You promised." Harold eyed the tree line. Somewhere in there was Elizabeth. The Elizabeth he had just met in the Gateway Travel Plaza was an avatar. Harold could not stop thinking about the woman in the black dress, the Quaker from Philadelphia, the woman who took his jaw in her hand and searched his eyes with hers in a way that melted something inside him. The woman he very much wanted to see again.

Harold looked back at the Gateway, infrastructural evidence that he was in his own time. But what did he have in his own time? Harold paused, taking quick inventory of his life. The future here held nothing he wanted to see again, including a bourbon-drinking FBI agent named Wong (or Wu) and a girlfriend who had clearly cut all ties.

Future employment? Probably making license plates or picking up roadside litter wearing canvas pajamas.

The uncertainty of what lie ahead elsewhere was something he chewed on. He had already been shot at, clobbered over the head, and tossed like a doll in a highway pile-up. But Harold felt his survival of those moments instilled boldness more than fear. He remembered the phrase "bloody but unbowed." *Hell yeah.*

A scream blew apart the somnolent air at the flea market. It came from the convenience store. A crashing sound followed. Then another, louder. All eyes lifted to the highway as the front doors of the store burst open with a bang. What emerged was hard for Harold to register at first.

Four British soldiers stormed from the convenience store, carrying a teenage girl. African American, and a store employee, based on her work vest. Two of the men grasped her arms in front while two had a leg each. She would have been face down, but she stretched her neck upright to be heard in full-throated outrage.

"Motherfucker! You try to rape me, I'll bite your dick off. I swear to God!" She bared her teeth and made snapping noises. "You in the terror now. I swear to God, you in the terror now."

The furiously squirming girl was dragged to a grassy spot and forced onto her back as other Redcoats began to gather in a circle around her.

At the flea market, customers looked to each other for direction. Harold could only shake his head in disbelief. None of this made any sense. *But*, he thought, *welcome to my life.*

The view was blocked as the Redcoats, wiping saliva from their lips, crowded in around the girl. A sense of helplessness prevailed among the onlookers, but Harold suddenly felt a pang of righteousness. He could hardly explain why, but he found himself walking in the direction of the British soldiers. He had no idea what he was going to do. He guessed he was going to punch somebody in the nose. *Yeah.*

He had taken several strides when a sound rose behind the crest of the highway. Horses' hooves, growing louder by the second. The Redcoats heard it, too, as did the flea market crowd. The clustered beating of galloping mounts increased until, emerging over the crest of the highway were men, and more men, comfortable on their mounts, a gray-clad army in leather gloves and hats. They reined in after arriving in front of the Redcoats, keeping their restive horses under control. The bearded officers in front in rakish hats, leather gloves, and sabers at their side impatiently surveyed the scene.

General J.E.B. Stuart lifted his plumed cocked hat and wiped his brow with a rag, then readjusted the hat. Satisfied that he was presentable, he turned his attention to the British officer.

"Who, may I ask, am I addressing here?"

The British officer sighed in exasperation. "Make way, make way. We have no business with you. Let the king's fusiliers pass."

A Confederate officer saddled on a horse next to Stuart pushed his hat back and spat.

"My, my, it's the king's fusiliers, Jeb. Sounds mighty highfalutin' to me. Should we skedaddle?"

Stuart, smiling, set his jaw and said nothing.

"Well now," said the Confederate officer, "I wonder if the king knows what kind of shenanigans these fusiliers of his are up to. My granddaddy called them lobsterbacks."

The British officer interrupted. "This grows tiresome. Give way to my men or you will suffer the consequences. I have no patience for Colonial upstarts."

Stuart wiped his brow again.

"We can parley," he said. "But first, release the girl."

With toxic grins, two of the British tightened their grip on the teen, whose fury rose a notch. "The first dick I see is a Slim Jim." She snapped her teeth again.

It was all a source of amusement to the British officer. "I have no inclination to give such an order," he said. "And my men take orders only from me."

Stuart's steed paced back and forth, but his eyes remained on this martinet also perched on a horse.

"I think you might want to reconsider those inclinations of yours. They might get you into a peck of trouble."

The Confederate officer turned his horse so he could, sotto voce, address Stuart face to face.

"Jeb, Ewell's waiting on us at Gettysburg. Remember Lee's orders?"

Stuart gazed to the east and stroked his chin. Then, the British commander broke the spell.

"Your intransigence leaves me few options. It was not my intent to bring force of arms to bear over such a trivial matter, but I am afraid you have left me without alternatives. The consequences are on your head."

He drew and raised his sword.

"Men, arms to port!"

The British snapped to attention and raised their muskets and rifles diagonally across their chests.

"Ready!"

The muskets were instantly lifted to shoulders and pointed at the Confederates, who struggled to control their startled mounts. The rebel horsemen pulled carbines from saddle holsters. Stuart brought up his LeMat revolver.

The men's eyes had turned to flint, a stone capable of sparks, but mostly just a cold, hard gray. All cards were flung to the table. Who would reach for the pot first? Someone had to.

For a moment, all was quiet except for the snorting of horses and clattering of their hooves. No order to fire had been given, but each man had picked a target and drawn a bead. The abducted girl had grown slack with fear and her slender hands now covered her mouth. Harold and the crowd at the flea market were nailed to the ground, eyes agape, mouths working.

This hair-trigger moment, guns drawn and pointed from two sides at close range across a girl who, on hands and knees, choked out sobs, seemed frozen in time.

A new sound arose.

Internal combustion engines in all their blub-blub and yak-yak were arriving imminently. Lots of them. Motorcycles coughed and growled as they rode into view. The riders, all men, pulled up to the scene, threw their booted legs out, and dialed the roar down to a rumble.

Nearly thirty motorcycles were in the unnatural state of being motionless with riders aboard and legs astride the asphalt. Their heavily tattooed riders wore their hair in a wide variety of configurations—on their necks, chins, and lips, straight or in braids. Greasy locks flowed down under Prussian spiked helmets and over tank goggles. Cigars smoke protruded from clenched teeth. One rider wore a pioneer woman's bonnet. Another had strung a pile of leis around his neck.

There were guns. Rifles in scabbards, Glocks in holsters and shotgun butts protruding from saddlebags. With almost comic leisure, the grinning riders gathered weaponry into their hands and checked their loads as they surveyed this peculiar situation that lay before them.

The Brits had become the meat in a biker-rebel sandwich. Anxiously, some turned to face the bikers. Their ranks were coming apart. The commander's horse sidestepped nervously. The commander snapped a thong against its flanks as he turned to his men.

"Back in ranks, you miserable ..."

Abruptly, a Chevrolet Impala careened up and squealed to a stop. Both doors flew open and a middle-aged black couple emerged, the man leading the way. He wore an Italian knit shirt with the paneled front over jeans and a stingy brim fedora with a plaid band. His face, a rictus of anger, he held his hands in fists that twisted back and forth at his side. The woman, adorned in stretch pants and a cotton pullover, storm clouds in her eyes, passed a raised index finger with monumental indignation in front of the face of the British soldiers she encountered.

The man elbowed soldiers aside and withdrew the captive girl. She folded into her father's arms. He whispered in her ear, put an oaken arm around her shoulder, and began to lead her away. The girl suddenly stiffened and pushed away. She walked back to one of the British soldiers and spat in his face.

"Ofay, motherfucker."

She patted her hair as she sauntered back to her father.

The bikers paused to remove cigars, grinned with yellow teeth, and spat on the asphalt. One of the bikers, gazing straight at Stewart, raised his elbows high and pressed his fists together. Stuart's men grinned, as if amused by the greeting. One lit a cigar and winked at the bikers.

Stuart mopped his brow, placed his feathered hat against his chest, and rolled his eyes skyward.

"Dear heart, Virginia now seems so distant. This Pennsylvania is full of the most ignominious individuals it has been my misfortune to cross paths with."

The British were now filing along the berm, eyes forward.

A Confederate officer pulled his horse alongside Stuart.

"Let's go find Ewell."

Stuart planted his hat on his head, nodded, and yanked on the reins of his steed.

With a "Hee-ya!" the Confederates thundered off past the Shell station, on their way to Gettysburg.

The bikers motored up and fell into ranks. "Limey cocksuckers," one shouted, as they passed the fusiliers.

On a ridge above the highway, the two Indians on horseback gazed down on what they clearly understood to be a warrior pageant, even though they had no understanding of the participants or the stakes. Without a word, they turned their mounts to leave.

Harold returned to the flea market where it was business as usual. The realization that the events he'd just witnesses had been visible only to him. As he contemplated this notion, a voice piped up. A woman wanted an explanation regarding a Shirley Temple cream pitcher she'd been scrutinizing. "This is out of whack," she said.

Harold tried to see his situation from a perspective that ignored the fact that it was inexplicable. He was alone, with no one to confront. He felt outrage, but where could he go with his beef? Who really cared? As far as he could tell, nobody. His outrage was deeply absurd, a tantrum in a closet.

He was suddenly reminded of a class he had taken years ago in college on twentieth century literature. The class had read Kafka's *The Trial* and devoted an hour to discussing the parable of the doorkeeper.

In the parable, a "man from the country" came to the court in the city to seek justice. He was stopped at the door by the doorkeeper, a shabby man wearing a flea-infested coat, who made him wait and implied the length of the wait was indeterminate. Year after year, the doorkeeper kept him waiting on a chair with vague promises; he even accepted a bribe so the petitioner could not dispute that he had tried every avenue. Eventually, death drew near, and the exhausted petitioner had a question: Why was he the only one seeking to enter this door to the court? Others certainly needed the court, needed justice.

As death hovered, the petitioner felt the doorkeeper draw close and heard him reveal the truth: the door was for him alone.

So this Breezewood, where time was a tossed salad, was for Harold alone. It was, at least, a frame of reference to work with. Maps were useless now. Navigation was neither vertical nor horizontal, but dimensional. If, to be sure, navigation was even possible in any direction.

Harold looked back to the parking lot in front of the Gateway Travel Plaza and saw that the FBI had returned, now with three black Suburbans. Agents piled out and Harold recognized Wu in a windbreaker, giving instructions to men who trotted in this or that direction. They ignored the flea market for now.

The tree line was across the highway. Harold need only wait for traffic to clear. Keeping to the right was the slow traffic, which included men and women on horseback and Conestoga wagons drawn by horses, mules, and oxen. Motorized vehicles passed on the left. The creak and rumble of iron-shod wagon wheels was offset by the muted hum of laboring cylinders. The many sounds of propulsion were in harmony across a ribbon of landscape. They signaled the promise of destinations whose cosmic and prosaic shapes were multitudinous. *Just pick one*, Harold thought. *It's the American way.*

He'd had enough of the traffic.

Jesus, did Americans never tire of this? You couldn't go from one place to another without dodging people headed somewhere else. It was amazing people stayed out of each other's way. I am getting grumpy, he thought.

Harold entered the tree line and, back in the woods, he was once again in a place without time signifiers or even evidence that man has been here. His eyes and ears were on alert. A directional arrow of some kind would appear. Of that he was certain. *Little else is certain,* he thought.

12

The sound came first, scraping noises followed by thumps. Scrape, whump. Someone was digging. Harold listened again. Maybe two shovels at work. Harold reached the edge of a clearing and, peering from behind a tree, absorbed the sight before him.

Two men were digging a hole that looked exactly like a grave. Nearby was, apparently, a body wrapped in a shroud of filthy canvas and trussed with hemp rope. Only the men's heads were visible, bobbing up and down as they scooped soil with shovels and flung it up and onto a large pile on the surface. Harold surmised they were almost finished.

Further into the clearing were two vehicles from different centuries. The contrast was almost absurd.

The first, a prairie schooner, a wagon with a canvas cowl. Two oxen placidly chewed on grass nearby. Harold saw that one of the wagon wheels had a broken spoke. A short distance away, a woman in a bonnet, her back to Harold, washed clothes in a tub, occasionally holding dripping items up to examine.

The second vehicle Harold recognized as a 1949 Hudson. A gleaming brown, cigar-shaped car, it looked like it was hurtling forward even when motionless. A man wearing jeans and boots, with a plaid flannel over a white T-shirt, stood with his back against the Hudson and smoked a cigarette, his attention focused on the men in the trench.

Harold tried to get a better look. He stepped into the sunlight at the very moment one of the men in the trench, who was wearing sunglasses, looked his way.

"We got company!"

All the faces turned toward Harold. The woman dropped her laundry, grabbed her skirt, and hustled to the back of the wagon, where she retrieved a shotgun and took aim at Harold.

"You best raise your hands high and come on out here," she said.

Harold complied and began walking forward with hands high. He soon reached the edge of the grave and looked down at the two laborers. In a moment, he was flanked by the woman and the man with a cigarette.

"Are you the law?" asked one of the men in the grave as he began to clamber out. He wore a loose-fitting shirt over canvas pants and boots. He brushed dirt from his clothes as he confronted Harold, head tilted to the side as he gazed cautiously at the intruder.

"I am not the law," Harold answered.

"Are you alone?"

"I am."

"Are you carrying a weapon?"

"No. I'm just a traveler. Can I lower my hands?"

The man in the canvas pants glanced at his wife, who nodded, and signaled at ease to Harold, who dropped his hands to his side.

An uneasy silence descended. The number of questions that arose from stumbling onto a burial deep in the woods were so many Harold decided upon an altogether different tactic.

"Nice car," he said.

The smoking man flipped his butt away. "My partner and I ..." he gestured to the man in the sunglasses still in the trench "...are delivering it to San Francisco."

He hooked a thumb at his broad chest. "I'm Sal. The man with the shovel is Dean."

Sal had the confident demeanor of an athlete. His shoulders supported a big, square head topped with barely combed black hair. Something seemed to be jumping in his eyes, as if he was already thinking three moves ahead.

Dean, dressed in jeans and a T-shirt, all dirt encrusted, hoisted himself out of the grave. He placed the shovel on his shoulders behind his head and grasped both ends. He began twisting casually from side to side as a smile, hinting at some wickedness, emerged on his face.

"You probably wonder what we're doing here," Sal said.

"Maybe it's none of my business."

"It's best you know. We're burying a man we killed. A man who deserved to die." Sal waited for a reaction, got only Harold's blank face, and continued.

"He tried to rob us!" The man in the canvas pants wiped his mouth after the outburst. "The son of a bitch! He was a flat-out son of a bitch robber! A stone bandit. Yessir."

Sal's wife folded her arms and nodded vigorously.

"This man is Efraim," Sal said, by way of introduction to the gravedigger. "We saw him repairing his wagon and pulled over to help. Then this wigged-out character and his googly eyed partner ran up with guns pointed and demanded the money box. This one got shot, the other ran."

"Who shot him?" Harold instantly regretted asking the question, but Efraim smiled and gestured to the wagon.

"Horace, show yourself."

A face, smoking a long clay pipe, poked out from the wagon's canvas. He brushed hair from his eyes and gazed placidly at the assembly. Harold guessed he was no older than fourteen.

Efraim walked over to the wrapped body. "Let's get this feller in his grave. His soul is surely transmitted, wherever it was headed, and it's left to us to bury his remains. Lord, lord, lord. Mmm, mmm, mmm."

13

With the body covered in tamped-down dirt, the men walked to a tub to wash, then sat on logs as Efraim's wife, Sarah, handed each a tin plate and filled it with beans, topping it off with a hard biscuit. Dean made a show of scratching his stomach and stretching before settling down to eat. The man was like a coiled spring, someone expecting trouble every minute, and Harold wondered if he had ever done time in prison.

Sal pointed his spoon at Harold. "Are you a madman? I need to know. Times demand to know. How is your brain wired and who, or what, is it wired to?"

"I beg your pardon?"

Sal chewed and swallowed. "You running *to* something or *away* from something? Doing something crazy? There's something behind the music. Wiggy stuff. Maybe you hear it."

Harold considered that. "Away from something, I guess. I have nowhere to run." He took a bite of the biscuit, which fell into flavorless shards in his mouth.

"That's cool. Consider only what's in front of you. Leave go of what's behind. Your life's an empty page, man. You can fill it any way you want. Cut a swath. Make history. Even fail spectacularly. In the end, man, have no regrets. Keep hold of your grace. Grace is all you got in the end."

Harold was still at "empty page." "How are you filling yours?" he asked.

Sal set down his plate and wiped his mouth with the back of a hand.

"That's hard to pin down. So far, at least. See, Dean and I live a life ruled by inertia. Whatever is moving tends to keep moving. We just keep on rolling under the stars. Where are we going? Everywhere, man, everywhere."

Dean nodded and grinned. "Dig it." He made a rocket sound and threw his head back and arms out. Sal chuckled.

"When you gotta haul ass, Dean's the man to be with. He's got this hammer. Well, really, it's a little sledgehammer. We get in a bind and some unruly cat gives us grief, Dean's there flipping that hammer. It tends to solve … problems."

Dean walked to the Hudson, reached inside and came back with a half-filled gallon jug of burgundy wine. He unscrewed the cap, rolled the jug to the top of his wrist, and lifted it to his mouth. His big Adam's apple jugged up and down. He passed the jug to Sal, who repeated the process, then offered it to Harold, who also partook.

Harold hailed Efraim, who was playing cards with his family, including a girl of about eight, and held up the jug. Efraim demurred and held up his own ceramic jug.

After another few rounds of the burgundy, Harold said, "I got a problem you might be able to solve."

Sal and Dean gazed steadily at him.

"I need a ride out of here."

Sal pressed his hands together and raised them to his lips. "No. That we cannot do, man. We got a rule. No passengers. It's just that when we're in the car, just the two of us, we got this karma going. We're madmen burning infinite rubber on boundless asphalt to an uncertain destination. An extra wheel won't hack it. Sorry, man."

Dean chimed in. "If you had tits, different story." His grin was criminal.

Sal rolled his eyes, hit the jug again, and screwed the cap back on. He rose and gestured to Dean, who also stood. Harold did likewise. The three brushed the seats of their pants.

Dean pulled out a pack of Camels, placed one between his lips, and gave one to Sal. Harold declined an offer and the two lit up.

After a moment of silence, Harold gestured to the Hudson. "Really is a nice car."

"Yeah, too bad it ain't ours. Like I said, we're driving it to Frisco for a friend," Sal said.

"Except he won't be our friend for long, once he sees that right front fender," Dean said.

Sal shrugged. "Our claws are sharper than his." He turned to Harold. "We gotta beat it."

With that, the two climbed into the sleek beast that had its heyday during Eisenhower's presidency. Dean took the wheel and gunned the big six to life. In a few seconds, they were gone, the sound of their radio going full blast trailing behind.

Harold walked over to Efraim and his family, who continued playing cards. "Sounds like you folks had yourself quite a day," he said.

"That's so. Horace, here, killed his first man." Efraim glanced at the boy, who knitted his brow. "Ain't nothing to be proud of, but nothing to regret, either. The man was a reprobate. Wretches like him invite an untimely end."

The boy flicked his eyes at his father, then resumed studying his cards.

"Tonight," Efraim continued, "I will take up the quill. I had promised those we left behind I would report all hazards we encountered, and I can only hope for the integrity of the carriers that can transmit this news. Generally, the folks we have crossed paths with have been plain dealers, most scrupulous in their accounting. But, today we encountered two scoundrels, poor toads who no doubt fell into bad company and took up arms as highway thieves. They met their match, as every mother's son traveling west is armed and on alert for vagabonds with ill intent. Such was my son, who made short work of one of them."

Efraim paused and looked at his son, who still puffed on his pipe as he listened to his father with mild interest.

"We will have our wheel fixed tomorrow. Our food stocks are good. We will be reunited in Pittsburgh with our caravan. I believe our obstacles may then become Indians who are unfit for social or civilized life or any of the moral culture we hold dear. All God-fearing men who confront the Indian do so with dread and anxiety. However, the native must give way as Scripture dictates. It is a law of nature that they should. If not, as regrettable as it could be, the force of arms will be brought to bear."

Efraim unholstered a revolver from his belt and held it up.

"Samuel Colt made this weapon, but it is God's hand that steadies our aim. Not everyone we encounter on our journey will be congenial, and conflicts may arise with both the Indian and white man, but righteousness will be on our side when we bring to bear this final remedy."

As Efraim reholstered the pistol, Harold saw the black flies buzzing near the wagon and he picked up a fecal smell.

"You may have more to worry about cholera than Indians," he said.

Efraim and his family seemed not to hear as they returned to their card game.

14

Harold found the slave camp, now deserted with wet burned logs in a pit. He squatted and poked a charred log with a stick as it if held a clue he could use.

He walked until he reached the path where he awoke under a bush with the Indians gazing down at him. He spotted a feather and picked it up. Harold sat, back against a tree, and regarded the feather. Had he worn the proper hat, he might attach it.

In an instant, he was back on his feet. Hoofbeats. Harold found a limestone outcropping with a gap on the bottom that, after he was prostrate, provided a full view of the path.

A dozen horsemen charged past. Harold saw a noose attached to a saddle horn. Some men wore hoods with eyeholes. Each rider was armed. Slave catchers.

After the vigilantes passed and the hoofbeats faded, Harold stood and looked down the path. It was quiet, but not completely. Ahead of him, behind another set of limestone teeth, a small group of families emerged. Harold turned to face them.

15

Where Harold previously showed up each day to apply his desktop skills to ill-defined data that had no significance to the price of beer and chipotle chicken wings, nothing grew outdoors that was not originally drawn on a landscaping plan. Every tree was placed by a crew, probably Salvadorans who lived twelve to a house, under the direction of a crew boss following a plan created by a landscaping engineer. Some trees screened the swooping lawns or rain swales for flood control, and the others softened the parking garage entrances.

At his office park, minutes from Fort Meade and the NSA, an army of government contractors plied their trade, basking in the powerful grow lamp of government spending energy that emanates from that great sun, Washington, D.C.

Harold had the top down on his Porsche and he trolled for a parking space. Some old blues by Sonny Terry honked on his car stereo as he maneuvered into an open space. He cut off the engine, exited the car, and headed for the office entrance. After a few steps, Harold realized he'd forgotten to put up the car's top. He pressed a finger to his lower teeth, then removed it and continued to the office. *What the hell. It won't rain.*

As Harold walked through a warren of cubicles, a tubby man in purple and black suspenders jumped out to greet him, waving a paper, which he thrust into Harold's face.

"Okay, here's week seven. Look at the spread with Miami. Miami?"

Cubicle Man feigned masturbation. Harold thrust his hips rhythmically to harmonize. They made the O-face together and grunted.

"Exactly," Cubicle Man grinned. He quickly sobered up. "Wait a minute, did I just give you an edge? Why did I do that?"

Harold clapped his back. "It is your nature. You should quit giving rides to scorpions."

Cubicle Man raised his hand for a high five. Harold swung his paw, but purposely missed.

He blew a kiss to Cubicle Man, who turned his back, throwing an upturned middle finger over his shoulder.

"Trust me at your peril. Mwa ha!" Harold crowed.

The moment Harold was in his office, he had headphones on and was spinning in his chair to "Cross the Track" by Maceo and the Macks. A hand on his shoulder stopped the spinning and Harold looked up, blanching, to see his manager, Graves.

Graves, as usual, looked distracted. He glanced down at his hand as if surprised to find it on someone's shoulder, and quickly withdrew it.

"We need to interface," he said.

"You want to talk?" Harold asked.

"Follow me." With that, he turned and headed to his office, Harold keeping up behind and straightened his tie.

Graves' office was a jungle. Ferns, rubber plants, and unknowable flora, probably from places where blowguns were commonly used, lined the walls. Graves lowered himself into a leather chair and Harold sat across from the desk.

"Where are you on the research on arms sale criteria? Some tank wonk still wants to know." Graves squinted at a file on his desk and tossed it aside, templing his fingers and examining his wedding ring.

"Interesting you should ask," Harold said. "We've developed some new observation platforms that I am sure will yield results. We are awaiting State Department vetting. However, the intel we're roping in so far has clear ..."

Graves held up a finger. "In other words, in paper limbo. Well, we're going to shelve that."

"Okay."

"In fact, I'm handing it off to Peterson and Myers."

"Okay," Harold said, nonplussed.

"I've got something new for you." He placed both palms down on his desk, lowered his head, then raised it slowly until his eyes met Harold's. "We're going to fillet some fish."

Harold donned his best ready-to-get-serious face. Graves now laced his fingers behind his head and rocked back in his chair, which seemed able to move in any conceivable roll, pitch, and yaw.

"The boys over at Langley have hit pay dirt with some data-mining dinkus they cooked up. They are peeking over the transoms in the Kremlin as we speak. It's become a cross ref project now, between what they are pulling in and the communications data warehoused by the nonesuch fellas down the road in Meade."

"So, now we can learn ..." Harold left the sentence unfinished.

"What it amounts to is HR on Kremlin brass. Could be mucho useful for various kinds of leverage. It's a big fucking carcass now and needs the knives. They net the fish, we fillet it."

Harold picked up the au courant theme.

"Used to be we got fish like that from Polyakov. The Russians were being fed by Ames and Hanssen."

"Those days are over, Harold. No more messages left under a bridge at a park. Now some geek in Gaithersburg living on Hot Pockets and coconut water invents a worm and starts delivering this stuff."

Graves parted the fronds of a fern to look out his window.

"They spank us, we spank them. The story never changes." He scratched his chin, gazing at the parking lot grid below. "The main thing is that, for us in our humble cubes, the metrics have changed. We're beginning a new cadence in our contract. It's sunrise and the coffee is perking."

"And I'm wide awake."

An indulgent smile played across Graves' face. "Delivery is in

four months. We want an executive precis, followed by a database of
names. You'll be receiving the downloads."

"Okay if I store it on a flash drive? Could be useful."

Graves shrugged. He picked up a watering can and eyed a fern.
Harold knew it was time to go.

16

In front of Harold now, the line of slaves parted in before the limestone teeth, and Harriet Tubman emerged. She walked toward Harold, holding a revolver next to her leg.

"Like a bad penny, you keep turning up."

"Nowhere else to go."

"You a Quaker? They're the only white people I trust."

"Afraid not," Harold said. "I was raised by a Unitarian and a Catholic."

Harriet holstered her pistol and sighed.

"Even God's least might have some purpose. Mmm, mmm, mmm."

"Maybe I should have a gun."

"What in the Lord's name do you need a gun for?"

Harold considered that. "I'm an American."

"You a white man."

"Maybe you shouldn't hold that against me."

Tubman threw her head back and laughed.

Elizabeth arrived, put hands on hips, and eyed Harold.

"What arrival from wanton parts is this? Harold, thee are welcome if thee embrace our mission still. By now, thee have a good reckoning of our purpose."

"Here I am, wanton as ever. I seem to be part of your mission." *God help me.*

"He's saying he might find a gun useful," Tubman said, still taking Harold's measure.

Elizabeth brushed a lock of hair from her face. "I do not carry a weapon. It is proscribed among the Friends. But I find that guns are more trustworthy in the hands of our African brethren."

"You may have a point," Harold replied.

The slaves had shouldered their burdens and were back on the path north with Tubman in the lead.

Harold turned to Elizabeth. "Where are you headed?" he asked.

"In Christiana, which is two days travel, there is a house with free Africans and abolitionists. From there, we turn north if we are not called to Philadelphia."

"Vermont, I heard."

"Slavery is criminal in Vermont and we have friends there. Canada is also close."

"It looks like we're on a path together. What do you think about that?" Harold asked.

The implication was not lost on Elizabeth. She looked off into the forest, drew a breath, and snorted it out audibly. Their eyes met.

"Thy path has led thee here. How that is, I do not know, but I deem there is a reason."

She drew closer and placed a hand firmly on Harold's chest.

"We need men and women of vision who scorn any stake in the here and now. Human lives are at risk, and all else is ephemera." She gnawed on the inside of her cheek. "Many persons speak to our cause. They read *The Liberator* and heed the words of Mr. Garrison. But in the breach, they turn away. Their attendance to our cause persists only insofar as it costs them no sacrifice."

"Such as money," Harold offered.

"And time. And life itself."

Elizabeth lifted her arms and clenched her fists. Her face was beseeching.

"The chains of slavery bind both white and African. For whites, it is especially difficult to adhere to principles of justice that require sacrifice, even when that sacrifice smashes their own chains as well as those of the Africans."

Harold was rapt, adrift, conquered. Elizabeth's voice turned husky as she lowered her face but kept her eyes fixed on his. He realized he was in her thrall. This woman. This time. This mission. He belonged.

"My trust in thee rests upon a certain foundation. It is that I judge thee ready to dedicate your life to our cause. There is no small import to what I say."

Harold swallowed. Elizabeth gripped his hands tightly.

"These are the stakes," she said.

Harold looked into her eyes and realized stakes didn't matter. He just wanted to be at this woman's side. The urgency of this feeling was so intense, he felt tears coming on and his voice was a croak.

He pulled the flash drive from his pocket and held it up.

"This doesn't look like much, but it was going to be my second Porsche, my rag hauler on the Chesapeake, my club membership, my condo in Stowe. And my trophy wife. Or it was supposed to be."

 He tossed it into the woods. Harold knew the import would be lost on Elizabeth, but it mattered to him. He drew in a deep breath and exhaled slowly.

"So long, Amber. I have your racquet, your Babolat Aero, or whatever. I hope you get it back." He raked fingers through his hair and looked at a nonplussed Elizabeth. "Actually, she'd probably organize a fundraiser for you. She's a liberal Democrat and her dad's loaded."

Elizabeth knit her brow and folded her arms. She closed one eye.

"Thou could depart now and I would say Godspeed. But I think thee and I share an understanding of this depravity that must be scotched. The buying and selling of humans is a wickedness of the first water that infects the American soul. It entails even those not engaged in this despicable merchandising who, nevertheless, participate in lies, deceit, and inhumanity."

Elizabeth gripped Harold's arm.

"We must throw ourselves, our very bodies, upon this odious machinery, the gears and levers, and make it stop. Make it stop! There is no other way."

The ex-slave wagon train approached. Harold watched its arrival and clicked his tongue in uncertainty.

"I tried this already and it didn't work. I go places in time, but geographically ..."

"Much depends on your faith."

"Faith?" He smiled. "Not really my frame of reference. In my upbringing ..."

Again, Elizabeth gripped his jaw and turned his face to hers. Once again, he melted.

"Whatever there was before, whatever will come later, all depends on what thee does now."

"Now?" Harold asked.

"Now."

As she halted the wagon train, Harriet Tubman echoed Elizabeth's response. "Now," she said.

Harold and Elizabeth climbed aboard and found seats among the slaves as the wagons rumbled back into motion. They left the clearing and rolled into the meadow he'd recently left. The travel plaza as he knew it was all just grass now, undulating in a gentle wind.

"Gateway," Harold muttered.

17

A tennis racquet, a Babolat Pure Aero, arced through the air in a powerful downswing and smashed the nylon-covered ball. It rocketed past the net into the far corner, leaving a bald man with a sunburned head lurching in vain.

"Game, set, match!" Amber performed an impromptu hip-shaking dance, holding her racquet high. She left the court, spinning her racquet like a baton twirler before planting herself on a bench next to Harold who briefly applauded and then returned to his cell phone. He was soon engrossed.

Amber mopped her face and neck with a towel and took a long swig from a brushed aluminum water bottle. She glanced at Harold's phone.

"Microcap or ultramicro?" she asked.

"Micro."

"Palo Alto?"

"New York."

"Ooh, old school."

"It's called market maturity."

"Cybersecurity?"

Harold rolled his eyes. "Well, that would be Palo Alto, wouldn't it?"

"Maybe not. Startups are right here in Maryland. Been on Route 270 lately?"

Harold summoned a patient smile for this woefully uninformed young woman.

"Biggest parking lot on the East Coast. Yes, I have spent many happy hours playing with my dick or almost getting killed on 270. Last week, I saw a Suburban on its roof."

Amber snorted, cackled, and pounded her racquet on the bench. She always said it was Harold's sense of humor that hooked her.

He went falsetto. "Gee, we must be in Maryland, Toto. There's Auntie Em and Uncle Buttfuck and …"

"Here come the flying monkeys!" Amber stifled a giggle with her fist.

"Surrender, Dorothy!"

Amber capped it with a witchlike, "Hee, hee, hee. And your little dog, too."

As a team, they swaggered into the clubhouse, where the air conditioning draped their glowing skin in a blanket of refreshment. Amber had the racquet behind her neck, one hand on each end, and switched from side to side as she smiled upon the wealthy and steadfast and the refined here in this Anne Arundel gin-and-tonic wet dream. The yachts of Annapolis were not far.

Waves and fist bumps greeted their entrance as they moved through the dining room to the bar. Their arrival at the bar summoned the bartender immediately. Grinning, he clasped his hands, laced fingers outward, and snapped knuckles while awaiting instructions.

Harold cocked his head. "Sapphire martini. Up. Three olives."

"Dry?"

"Point the gin bottle at France."

"Sounds illegal."

"I'll take the rap."

"And the lady?"

The routine always amused Amber. "France sounds good," she smiled. "A glass of Pouilly Fuissé."

Amber was now absorbed in her own cell phone as they eased into stools that not only had padded backs, but also padded armrests. Harold gazed at a bar menu.

"Wanna do crabs at Cantlers?" *~ ANNAPOLIS !*

He waggled his eyebrows. Suggesting crabs was kind of a dare. At least in Maryland. Dare you say no?

"Honey, I'm in my whites." She looked up from her phone. "Plus, it's a half-hour drive. Plus, you can't even get into the parking lot on a weekend."

Their drinks arrived. Harold sipped, allowing the ice-cold gin to revive his ambition for weekend fun.

"So, Bethesda again?"

"I like Bethesda."

"A hundred trendy restaurants. What's not to like?"

They sipped again. Amber made a show of closing down her phone, placing it on the bar and turning to Harold.

"Harry, we have to talk."

"That's what she said."

"What is the next step for us?"

"Well, we have a decision to make," he deadpanned. "Refills here or head to Bethesda?"

Her voice lowered to a sharp hiss. "Will you stop being a wise-ass for once?"

Harold tossed off the last of his martini and signaled for another. He swiveled his stool to face Amber and cleared his throat.

"Amber, what if the rules change? What if I can make them change? What if I break a certain rule and it rocks our world?"

"What rules?" She was immediately on guard.

"What if all bets are off?"

"Bets? What the fuck are you talking about?"

"What I'm saying is, let's forget the past. Let's focus on the future."

She drained her wine and also signaled for a refill. "Forget the past? Harry, do you have something to tell me?"

"All will become clear soon. I am about to open a door, a very lucrative door I may add, and make manifest my glorious destiny."

She snorted. "So go open the door. It's over there. Try not to piss on your shoes."

18

The sun arose on the caravan of slaves, who had been riding all night, taking turns sleeping and keeping the horses on the move. They trundled into a clearing. Time for high alert.

Harold had been laying on burlap sacks with a straw hat over his face. He awoke and removed the hat to see that the wagon train was slowing. Two men on foot stood on the trail ahead of them.

Harold sucked in his breath in recognition of Daniel and Jamal from the hippie van.

He stood up in the wagon. "Whoa! Whoa!"

The wagons lurched to a stop and Harold jumped out of his wagon to greet these unrepentant troublemakers. His kind. They embraced.

"Hey, you have some sense of timing," Daniel said.

Harold looked them over. "Just you two?"

Daniel shrugged. "Tanya is ... how do you say it? Still on

patrol."

The trio came to grips with it. Then Daniel smirked at Harold.

"Are you one of those 'victims of the contemporary malaise?'"

Harold chuckled. "Yeah, well, the Port Huron Statement was my bedtime story. You met my parents."

"I think that right now Jamal and I have a lot of that fuckin' malaise."

Jamal, whose arms had been folded, raised his hands to point double digits at Harold and Daniel.

"Fuck malaise. You two white boys go ahead and pig wallow in your fuckin' malaise. You see before you a black man from west Baltimore. We didn't have no malaise. We were lucky to have toast and mayonnaise."

He played an air guitar riff, then moved his hands in close like a hypnotist.

"Cops, judges, probation officers all be like, Army will straighten you out, nigger. You need discipline. Hell, what they're saying is, 'You need the whip.'" He worked his jaw. "Mmm. Mmm. Mmm."

Harold turned to see Elizabeth, Harriet, and the rest regarding this scene with curiosity.

"It's okay," he told them. "These men are in our army."

—

Dawn the next day came and went, and the slaves' caravan had been on the move two hours as the sun lifted into the treetops. Harold, Jamal, and Daniel shared a wagon with two escaped slaves, Henry and Napoleon.

Jamal turned to the black men across from. "Where you folks from?"

"We both from a plantation in Frederick," replied Henry Harris.

"Frederick? That in Virginia?"

"It's in Maryland."

Jamal calculated, scratching his chin. "How far away from here?"

"About forty miles."

"And, uh, when did you make your departure?"

"We run off three days ago."

"So ...." Jamal was lost in thought over the speed of slaver vigilantes on horseback pursuing a poky wagon train. He didn't like the odds.

Harold stepped in.

"We're headed for a place called Christiana. We'll get there before nightfall. It is a homestead with whites and free blacks."

"And from there?" Jamal inquired.

"They're telling me Vermont."

"Next door to Canada, I like that."

19

As the wagons rounded a bend, the eyes in each vehicle snapped to attention. Two figures stood in the middle of the road. One was a slave named David Harris, whose hands were tied behind him. The other was a white man in a stovepipe hat with a gold-tinted vest over his vast belly. He stood behind David, gun against David's head.

"Hold up there!" the armed man insisted.

The wagons creaked to a stop.

The man in the towering hat spoke, shouting his words like a preening carnival barker.

"My name is Edward Gorsuch. I am a citizen of the state of Maryland and I have in my possession a warrant sworn out by Judge William Dupree of Frederick County for the arrest of slaves who recently fled from my farm. I could read you the names of the slaves, but you know the names and ..."

He pulled the hammer back on his revolver with a click.

"This here's one of them."

On either side of the trail, the undergrowth rustled and more than a dozen men emerged, all with guns drawn. One wore a noose around his neck like a scarf. Two wore bags over their heads with eyeholes cut out. Those who didn't hide their faces wore a depraved grin of lordly triumph over the misbegotten.

Elizabeth stood up in her wagon and folded her arms.

"We are in Pennsylvania. This is a free state."

Gorsuch bugged his eyes playfully and woofed, and the laugh was picked up by his men.

"Well, now, I imagine that might have counted for something last year, except the law has since changed." He held up the warrant. "This here's the law speaking, young lady."

"Take us before a Pennsylvania judge," Elizabeth demanded.

Gorsuch's face darkened.

"Well, I reckon that's what you would like. Yes, I reckon so. Get one of your Quaker friends on the bench to pound his gavel and order these slaves released." Gorsuch turned to his crew. "What say you, boys?"

The vigilante with the noose swung it over his head as the others cheered. Brandishing a revolver, he approached the wagon with Harold and the others.

"Boss, you hit the jackpot. We got ourselves your niggers, someone else's niggers, some nigger-loving white boys, and their nigger-loving Quaker friends. We get this wretched crew back to Maryland and you shall be Queen of the May."

Laughter rippled through the Gorsuch crew.

Noose Vigilante rode his horse over to another wagon and surveyed the women inside, one of whom was Harriet Tubman, tucked into a corner of the wagon and covered with a shawl. Her hand emerged from the shawl, revealing a revolver which she immediately fired. The bullet hit Noose Vigilante in the center of his forehead. His eyes rolled up, as if he wanted to see the point of impact, before he toppled out of his saddle and hit the ground with a dust-raising thud.

After a shocked silence during which nothing happened, Harriet thumped the wagon driver on the head.

"G'wan."

She turned her gun on the astounded slaver holding David hostage and shot him through the chest. The man gave out a whoop and stumbled into the bushes where he collapsed and remained still. David ran to the back of the wagon and was swiftly hauled aboard. The wagons clattered down the path, drivers shouting at the horses. The men on the escaping wagons withdrew weapons and opened fire at the scattering vigilantes as they tore down the lane.

But one wagon, the last of the lot, was left behind. Weaponless and blocked in front by adversaries with cocked guns, those within the wagon raised hands in surrender.

Gorsuch sauntered over, his face radiating outrage, his gun covering them. His finger stroked the trigger.

"Uh-huh, uh-huh, uh-huh. Well now, what kind of lowlife miscreants are these that stand before us now?"

Daniel stood in the wagon. "Fuck you and the horse you came in on."

"Shoot that cocksucker," Gorsuch ordered casually.

One of the slavers raised a pistol with a gleeful expression.

"Wait!" Harold cried. "This man can be ransomed!"

Gorsuch waved away the slaver and his gun. "The hell you say."

"The hell I *do* say." Harold's mind raced. "He is the son of a wealthy family of New York merchants. He is currently fleeing from his responsibilities back home, including a woman who he, um, left in a family way."

Gorsuch squinted, assessing the bait. He removed his stovepipe and smoothed the silk lining. "Tell me, why would a good Christian family welcome back a reprobate like this, much less pay good money in ransom to save his hide?"

"He's not a Christian. He is of the Jewish faith."

Daniel held a sullen expression as Gorsuch approached to have a closer look.

"A Hebrew?" Gorsuch gestured to one of his men. "Take down his pants."

Two men pulled Daniel from the wagon and one yanked down his trousers. Gorsuch inspected, stroking his jaw.

"Where you headed, Jewboy?"

"I don't have to answer to goyim scum like you."

Gorsuch gestured to a man with a whip. "Give him a taste."

The grinning man lifted lips over his three teeth and hit Daniel on the back with the lash. That was that.

"Okay, a cotton ship leaves Philadelphia for Liverpool in four days. My family owns the ship. The first mate is my cousin. We have friends in England."

Harold chimed in. "His family owns a lot of ships. They're rich fucking Jews."

Daniel bristled at this calumny. "Anti-Semite!"

"Daniel, I'm just trying to …"

Gorsuch planted his hat firmly back on his head. "Silence! What am I doing standing here listening to this folderol in this godforsaken territory they call Pennsylvania. Back to Frederick. Let's go!"

One of the vigilantes ordered the black wagon driver into the back of the wagon at gunpoint and took the reins himself. Another of Gorsuch's crew hopped onto the rear and trained his pistol on the men, finding a straw to chew on as he settled in.

In a moment, the wagon was again in motion, now following the rest of the posse on horseback. They were now headed south, toward Maryland. Toward slavery.

Harold and Daniel exchanged glances across the wagon while sharing the same thought. *What now?*

Jamal suddenly piped up. "I hear them Jewesses up in New York be right generous with their favors. That true?"

Daniel, circumcised because he was born in a military hospital, easily picked up the Jewish thread.

"There's a saying up there in New York. Among us yids," Daniel leaned forward conspiratorially. "You know how Jewish women hold their liquor? By the ears."

Laughter erupted from the whole crew.

The vigilante tonguing a straw bugged his eyes at this. Daniel grinned and bit the inside of his cheek. He winked. This talk was for men only.

"They like to pose for portraits, too. With nothing on!"

"Go on," Harold said.

"I swear this is no lie. I have some of these pictures, including one of poor Rachel, who, I fear, I have left with my progeny in her belly. She has an ungodly mound of bush on her mons veneris. But I lent her my razor and she shaved it off for this here picture."

He reached into a pocket and pulled out his hand as if cupping a photo in it. He held it over to Harold.

"Mmm. Mmm. Mmm," Harold said, gazing into the cupped hand. He licked his lips.

As a strained groan burst from his throat, the vigilante lunged for the photo, grabbed Daniel's wrist, and was startled to see Daniel's cupped hand was empty. He was off balance in an awkward crouch, an easy target. Daniel caught the man's jaw in a sharp right uppercut, followed by a roundhouse left hook that landed just below the ear. The straw fell from the man's mouth as his head lolled backward and the pistol rolled out of his hand. Jamal seized the gun and the three bailed out of the wagon and hit the dust running, disappearing into the underbrush.

The vigilante holding the reins watched, mouth agape, as the last of them darted behind a brace of trees.

"Well, shit."

20

At a safe distance in the woods, the men assembled.
With two different agendas, it was clear they would not stay together.
The slaves wanted to rejoin Harriet Tubman and Elizabeth to the east.
Harold, Jamal, and Daniel would head north. They shared hugs. One
of the slaves pointed to the revolver Jamal swiped from the wagon.
Jamal slapped the man on the shoulder and smiled, then shook his
head as he tucked the gun, now his gun, into his waistband. The two
groups separated.

Daniel was in the lead as the group of three headed to what
looked like north judging from the sun's late afternoon position. The
trail barely existed; they walked with eyes down.

Daniel paused and raised a hand.

"I smell something."

Jamal rolled his eyes. "I know. Funky, ain't it?"

Jamal rubbed his head. "Dandruff's comin' back, too. I could
really use a shower. In fact, I could really use a shower, followed by a
joint, a bottle of Dewar's and dinner with Aretha Franklin, followed

by ..."

Daniel, ignoring this, said, "Man, I know that smell."

They each sniffed the air curiously and resumed walking. The odor's identity gradually became evident. Cooking sour mash. A still.

Click!

The sound behind them was unmistakable and they slowly turned.

A man in overalls over a stained river driver shirt, wearing a ragged black hat with flopping brim and a hole in the crown, leveled a shotgun at them. Another man, wearing a barn coat, emerged from behind a tree in front of the men with a revolver pointed from the waist.

The shotgun toter kept Harold and company covered as the other frisked them, eventually finding Jamal's revolver.

"This here jasper's carrying a Colt, but I don't see any badges. I don't reckon they be revenooers. But the plain fact of the matter is, what the fuck are they doing here?"

"I reckon they are trespassing."

The two turned silent, letting the intruders speak.

Harold squinted at the man in front.

"Benny?"

Then he turned to the other man.

"Max."

He smiled. "We've met before."

Benny walked up to Harold and took in his face.

"You're that sorry-ass ragamuffin we picked up on our way to Mamie's."

"Met you at the Gateway Travel Plaza, too."

Benny sucked his teeth, then gestured forward with his gun.

"Walk ahead of us up yonder. I ain't inclined to flap my jaws out here."

The procession of five men continued down the path. They emerged into a clearing where a steaming whiskey still revealed itself as the source of the sour corn essence that drifted through the trees. Alongside were small barrels, jugs, and stacks of mason jars in boxes. Nearby was a firepit with logs to sit upon.

"Have a seat," Benny offered, still leveling the shotgun.

They each picked a log, including Max. Benny stood vigil behind them.

"Are we still in Pennsylvania?" Harold asked.

"I do believe," Max replied.

"What's the nearest town?"

"Chambersburg, I reckon."

"What about Breezewood?"

Max and Benny both cackled, and Benny answered. "Breezewood ain't no town. At least, nobody lives there. It's just for folks passing through to fuel up ... All kinds of fuel." He jammed his thumb toward the still.

Max picked up the thread. "You're the ones need to answer questions. Whatever reservation you belong to, you are plumb off it. What are you aiming to do here?"

Harold made the introductions. "This here is Daniel Bodine, a former staff sergeant in the U.S. Army, currently helping his friend, Jamal Weeks, who refuses to be drafted ..."

He extended a hand in invitation to Jamal to finish the sentence.

"...into a fucked up war in Vietnam," Jamal said.

"Indeed. Fucked up war," Harold resumed. "They are headed for Canada. We are currently, well, not to put too fine a point on it, lost."

Benny lit a pipe, squinting against the smoke, and when it was drawing right he reached into a box and pulled out a quart jar filled with clear liquid. He twisted off the lid, blew out a plume of smoke, and turned to Harold.

"You still blow that mouth harp?"

Harold produced the Hohner and held it aloft like a trophy. In the deepening night it captured the firelight and flashed as an instrument without any organic meaning outside the hand that held it and the mouth that caressed it. The others gazed at the mouth organ like a talisman whose value had only begun to be tested, holding a promise for something not yet known.

21

The velvet curtain of darkness had draped the surrounding woods but, around the firepit, crackling logs piled waist high cast a shivering light on the nearest trees. Shadows passed across them, too; shadows of men dancing around the fire. Each held a jar and took sips. Max and Benny were clogging, stomping in a lunatic mountain rhythm that involved knee slapping and elbow churning. Daniel tried to follow. Jamal had his own moves, arms akimbo, picked up, no doubt, somewhere in the clubs on Pennsylvania Avenue in west Baltimore.

Harold blew hard and urgently. It was Magic Dick's "Whammer Jammer," an E major foot propellant of uncanny persuasion.

Were the quintet to scrutinize the tree line in the shimmering light, they would detect two faces, each one on horseback. The Indians regarded the dancing men around the blazing fire stoically for a while, then cut their mounts and merged with the darkness. This was not of them, by them, or for them. But it was deserving of respect.

—

Harold, wrapped in a blanket, awakened in the clearing as daylight took hold. He was alone. The whiskey still and firepit were gone. He felt stiff from sleeping on the ground, as usual, but noticed he had no hangover. He headed back to the tree line. *Where else to go?* It seemed sleep or unconsciousness reset the clock and the tree line opened the door. *What's to await me next?* Harold wondered. Even the appearance of a stegosaurus would not amaze him.

As he emerged from the trees, Harold saw he was back facing the Gateway Travel Plaza, and he began the hike across the meadow and parking lot.

Harold noticed a building he hadn't seen before, a car rental agency called Go Now Rentals. He had rented plenty of cars. Could it be that simple? He immediately shifted direction and walked toward it. Except for the roof, the building was encased in glass. Not a single car was parked near it, which Harold found odd. Once indoors, he saw no one in the waiting lounge. No one was behind the counter, either. No sign of human occupation.

"Hello? Anyone here?"

At this, a door opened. A woman began to emerge when a summons from within caught her attention and she ducked back behind the door. She spoke, but the words were inaudible to Harold. Moments later, she emerged again and shut the door. She was tall, a bit lanky, her blonde hair in a chignon, and dressed in a uniform of sorts. She looked to Harold like a Pam Am stewardess in the Howard Hughes era.

She approached the counter, placed her hands on it, and then startled Harold by leaning far forward and pushing her face to within inches of his. Her widening grin and skyward eyebrows had a startling effect. He almost flinched, but then she relaxed and eyed him with amusement.

"My name is Serena. How may I help you?" It was if she was saying, "I got your number, pal."

Harold collected himself. "Well, I'd like to rent a car."

She gave a satisfied nod; the terms of their engagement had been set and she was ready to happily comply. Harold wondered if he could have asked for drugs or sex.

"You've come to the right place," she said.

"You'll want a credit card and driver's license, I suppose."

"Nope." She popped her lips at the end of the word.

Harold was taken aback while reaching for his wallet. "No?"

"You may qualify for Express Service."

"Express?"

"Yes, indeed."

Harold scanned the table and decided to play the ace.

"Yes, that's exactly what I want. Express Service. You give me a car and I drive it away. I just drive it the hell out of here. Yes indeed."

"First, however, we have to make sure you qualify."

"And what does that entail?"

Serena removed a clear plastic bag from behind the counter and carried it around to stand in front of Harold. Harold could see various medical instruments inside. Serina retrieved a tongue depressor and waved it in front of Harold's face until he caught on and opened his mouth. Her toothy smile reshaped into a moue of concentration. She depressed his tongue and shone a tiny flashlight into his mouth, tilting it to assess both upper and lower teeth. Then, controlling his face with a light touch, she shone the light in his eyes.

Serena clicked off the flashlight and dropped it back into the bag. She then tossed the tongue depressor into an empty wastebasket as she resumed her spot behind the counter.

"I'll skip the ear exam," Serena said. "You seem to be able to hear fine."

"Was that fun?" Harold asked.

She smiled.

"So, do I qualify?"

"One last thing. You must participate in our customer survey."

"You have questions."

"A little more than that. Come with me." Serena opened the door to the next room and motioned for Harold.

They entered a small alcove with an escalator leading down. Harold followed Serena's lead as they rode a long stretch of moving stairs to some unforeseen destination. Music played somewhere in the distance, and Harold recognized Neil Young's "Helpless." Stepping off the escalator, Harold found himself at one end of a vast garage with rank after rank of vehicles of every size, type, and vintage.

Some of the vehicles had hoods up and were being worked on. A horn signaled that a car was going up on a hoist. Off to one side, an eruption of welding sparks caught Harold's eye. Serena turned to him as they walked abreast down a central aisle and he turned his attention from this sheet metal spectacle back to her.

"I'll try to keep the process moving along," Serena said, with professional concern. "I am guessing you are a man who does not like to be kept waiting."

"Time is important," Harold smirked.

"Precisely."

He looked around at the epic array of internal combustion vehicles surrounding him.

"Y'know, I used to drive a Porsche."

"A pork?"

"No, a Porsche. It's a sports car."

"What happened to it?"

"I'm not sure. I …" Harold interrupted himself. "Where, may I ask, are we going?"

"There's someone you must meet."

Serena stopped by a bay with a 1969 GTO Judge. A man's legs stuck out from under it. "Maybe you should have had one of these."

Harold leaned back to admire this muscle monster, Pontiac's coolest move. He put a hand on the fender.

"You're probably right. Y'know, Pontiac's chief engineer was John DeLorean when this was built."

"And you bought some *Porch* car. What is that?"

"French. I think I was reading Albert Camus at the time."

Two bays down sat a cherry red 1957 Chevrolet Belair with a button-tufted interior and an open trunk. As Harold and Serena moved closer to examine the car, a man in a white jumpsuit slammed the trunk shut and glowered at them, running an ACE comb through his thick black hair. He snapped the bubblegum he'd been chewing."

The man had a square face with long eyelashes over a supple mouth. His pomade-infused hair plunged ahead over his forehead while sweeping backward on the side fenders. The man walked around the car and stood before Harold and Serena, legs slightly spread. He pulled a rag from a back pocket and, after plunging both hands into a can of lanolin, wiped his big digits, digging into the spaces between his fingers. He rocked gently on his heels.

Serena did the honors.

"Harold, this is Johnny. Johnny, Harold."

Johnny did a final wipe of his right hand on his thigh, and gripped Harold's hand. They shook in silence.

Johnny squinted at Harold and then, abruptly, threw both arms straight out like he was shooting his cuffs. He leaned his head to the right as he cocked a hip in the same direction, then snapped his hip to the left as his head rolled backward like a monk in ecstasy.

Johnny put his fingers to his temples and started rolling his eyeballs. He cocked his head and did the swami move once more.

"I'm sensin' somethin' here." His accent was deeply Southern. "Yeah, I feel the karma. I can dig it. This is heavy."

He snapped out a hip again and did a fast draw with his finger, aiming at Harold's chest.

"You got trouble and you're running out of time. Tell me I'm wrong."

"Time? Yeah, that's an issue. But really I just need a ride."

"Heard that one before. Everyone needs a ride. Gotta be someplace else. Gotta get out of here. Go, go, go. Old fucking story, man."

Johnny began to stride down the aisle in the sea of cars and Harold and Serena fell in behind.

Harold swept his arm. "You got cars galore here. Just let me have one."

Johnny made a clucking sound. "It ain't about cars. It's about righteousness. You dig?"

They soon reached a little office and went in. Crates of oil in quart cans filled one corner, an old metal Sinclair sign with a dinosaur hung on a wall. On a shelf, a huge parts catalogue lay open. The garage's gasoline odor permeated everything. The cardboard crates that held the motor oil in this tiny office had begun to rot.

Serena took a corner chair, opened her purse, and pulled out a manicure kit.

Johnny opened another jar of lanolin, extracted a blob with three fingers, and began massaging it into his hands. He opened a desk drawer and pulled out another rag to wipe his hands. Seated in a rusting swivel office chair, he threw his head back, laced his hands behind his head, and stared at the peeling wallpaper on the ceiling, from which dangled a fly strip bejeweled with dead flies.

"I'm figgerin'."

Johnny grinned as he examined an old pin-up calendar featuring a spunky redhead in a gas jockey cap next to a pump with the legend "Let us oil and grease it for you." He winked broadly at the faded photograph and took a couple of fast chews of his gum.

"I'm figgerin."

Suddenly, he jolted forward on his creaky chair, closed one eye, and targeted Harold with the other.

"You armed?"

"Not at the moment."

"Lemme see about that." Johnny pulled open a drawer on the scuffed desk and brought out a .357 Magnum revolver. He pulled out the cylinder to make sure it was unloaded, then closed the cylinder with a click. He brought it to his face and sighted down the barrel at the stack of oil cans.

"I know what you're thinkin'. Do ya need to shoot a bullet through an engine block? Well, do ya?"

Why?

Harold looked around this godforsaken grease monkey's office and felt despair beginning to consume him. *What is this place? Who are these people? Why am I here?* He looked over at Serena, who attentively filed her nails, an act that seemed to require her total concentration. Then his eyes fell on Johnny, who was again ogling the "oil and grease" calendar girl.

"I'm beginning to wonder if I want to shoot a bullet through anything, unless it's my own head," Harold said.

"Everybody wants somethin'. How about you?"

"I want to get out of here."

Johnny stood abruptly and combed his hair again. He walked in front of the chair. Serena, whose eyes were still downcast as she poked a cuticle, remained perched upon her seat.

Johnny suddenly snapped his posture in Harold's direction and pulled out two index fingers, pointing like pistols at Harold.

"Let's get one thing straight. I ain't got no magic wand. If I did, I'd wave it over my own damn head. You think this is where I wanna be? This ain't even a garage in some flyspeck in Mississippi, much less Memphis. I could drive thirty miles south of here, but then I ain't even in the South. I'm in Maryland or West Virginia."

The geographical reference lent some clarity to the discussion.

Johnny laced his fingers and cracked his knuckles. "Sorry, but that ain't the South. You ever had biscuits and gravy in Maryland? Tastes like bait. Anyway, what's the big deal where you are? It's all a pain in the ass."

Something rose inside Harold. Something that wanted him to make a fist, take a deep breath, and snort out his nose. So, that's what he did.

"Whatever life I got coming, and it might suck big time, it won't be in this godforsaken Twilight Zone waystation. I may be the victim of some kind of cosmic stunt. In fact, I sure as fuck am the victim of some cosmic goddamn stunt. But I'm not about to lie down and play sucker."

Johnny smirked. "You are beginning to tax my patience with your sorry-ass whining."

The indignation rose to Harold's scalp and he felt the heat in his face. He began to pace the tiny office.

"First of all, who the fuck are you? Who died and made you Pharaoh of Egypt? You're the boss of ... what? This?" His arm swept the office. "This is Hicksville, Pennsylvania, you Hicksville fucking hick! Do you think for a moment ..."?

Harold was looking in the wrong direction to see the blow coming. A sharp fist to the face snapped his head back and cut off his tantrum. Harold's hand cupped his nose and he lowered his head. Blood. Shocked, he took an unsteady step backward.

Johnny rolled his shoulders and rubbed his knuckles. He bared his teeth and inhaled with a hiss. Then, the knots of anger relaxed and his face turned serene.

"I so dislike violence. I dislike it intensely because it is an obstacle to communication. When you hit, you shut the door."

Serena paused her nail makeover long enough to hand Harold a semi-clean rag, which he pressed to his nose.

Johnny returned to his chair, placed an elbow on the chair arm, and his jaw in his hand. He pivoted back and forth with a rhythmic squeak.

"I grew up in Mississippi. Bacon drippins' and cornbread. And collards. And Sunday meetings. White folks' church was right next to the black folks' church, and we could hear that gospel music over in our church. Man, I'm tellin' ya, I wanted to be over in that church. Whoo-ee!"

Johnny's eyes focused on some distant happy vision of bare feet on red clay, a can of fishing worms, and pie smells wafting out the window. That's what Harold surmised, anyway.

"After services, the uncles would come over to my house with their hens in tow. You know what I mean. My dad had some Old Crow in the shed." Johnny laughed. "In fact, he had a *lot* of Old Crows in that shed. And he was always invitin' the uncles to come and see some new tool. They'd come back from the shed a little wobbly in the legs, like a raccoon. This was a life where a young man might stake a claim."

Johnny spread his hands. "So, what am I doing here in Pennsylvania? What did I do to deserve this?"

Serena abruptly stopped filing and looked up, catching Johnny's eye. Harold saw a merciless look.

Johnny caught the look and uttered a choking sound. He twisted the front of his jumpsuit in his hands and let out an agonized "Christ Almighty!"

Silence descended. Harold was nonplussed. There was only the scritch-scritch of the nail file as Serena returned to her efforts.

Johnny gathered himself and sighed. He turned to Harold.

"You gotta ask yourself something. It's not where you are, it's *who* you are. Who am I looking at here? What kind of man am I looking at? The kind that just takes and takes? Then stiffs his girl and cheats on his taxes and leaves a dollar tip? What did you do?"

A dam burst inside Harold and he hiccuped. Heat and liquid flooded his face, which was slowly turning side to side. Tears sprung from Harold's eyes and his chest spasmed with a long, wet inhaled sniff.

Johnny walked toward Harold and grasped the lapels of his jacket as if examining a new specimen of bug.

"Oh, boo, hoo, hoo. 'I want to go home. Please take me home.'" Johnny tapped Harold's face lightly. "Well, straighten up and be a man. You can't go home. No one wants you. No one cares. Your sorry ass has been tossed overboard." Johnny's face softened. "What was the last record you bought?"

Harold started to surface from his misery. "What?"

"I said, what was the last record you bought?"

"Well, I download music."

"Like what?"

"Some sides by Charlie Musselwhite and Sonny Terry. You know Magic Dick? J. Geils Band?" Harold blew his nose into the rag Serena had given him. He heaved in a big breath and took out the harp. He fit it in his jaw, cupped it in his hands, and started blowing "Hootin' Blues" by Sonny Terry and Brownie McGhee. The only thing missing was the train whistle.

A crowd gathered, mechanics wiping their hands on rags or adjusting their baseball caps. They tapped their dirty Chuck Taylors to the rhythm.

Harold closed the song with a final skronk to a smattering of applause. Serena even joined in.

Johnny had a pencil now and was tapping the eraser against his teeth.

"I'm gonna be straight with you, Harold."

"Okay."

"You can't leave."

Harold said nothing.

"Pay attention now. Ya see, you gotta be taken out."

"You mean like on a stretcher? Or a gurney?"

"No, man." Johnny paused. "Well, in fact, that's one way. But that's not what I mean. You gotta ... enlist."

"Like ... in the Army?"

"That's still not what I mean." Johnny gave it some thought. "How'd you get here?"

"I got stranded. That is, I had to get away from ... some people. I was on my way to ... somewhere. I ended up here when my car broke down. I've been trying to find a way out ever since."

"But you couldn't go forward and the door was locked behind you."

Harold considered, then nodded.

"You need a key for the next door. Y'see, someone's got to give you that key. I don't have it. I don't even know who does have it. But someone does, I guarantee. You gotta find that person."

Harold's shoulders slumped as helplessness stole in. "How does that even happen?"

"Is there anyone who needs your help?"

Harold shrugged. Johnny gave Harold's shoulder a soft punch, then threw an arm around his shoulders and led him out of the office. Serena put away her nail file, rose, pulled out a compact, flipped it open, and patted her chignon. Perfection. They headed down the aisle to the far end of the garage.

"Okay, listen up, my friend," Johnny said. "There's a way in here and a way out. This is second chance city, man. But sometimes it requires giving up something precious. You pay for the ticket, but it comes with no guarantees. You dig?"

Johnny stopped and gave Harold a gentle cheek slap. He put a finger under Harold's chin and lifted his face. Johnny took the gum out of his mouth, examined it, and returned it to his back molars for further mastication. His brows knitted as he returned attention to Harold.

"The board of transportation takes no responsibility for you arriving at your preferred destination. It's the hard truth, man, but what else can I tell you? Can you factor that?"

"Is this still the Express Service?"

Both Johnny and Serena laughed aloud. Serena turned to face Harold and spoke.

"You have a ways to go, young man. You have strong teeth and good eyesight. These will help. Put one foot in front of the other until you are on the right path. You'll know when."

They approached a door with an exit sign above.

"That's the way out, man," Johnny said.

The way out, Harold considered the words. *The exit. The. Way. Out. People spend their lives trying to find the way in and some do and some don't. Some regret it and some don't.*

Harold chose out. He turned to Johnny.

"Are you the gatekeeper?"

Johnny and Serena both erupted in laughter again. They high-fived each other. Johnny spread his legs, threw his head back, and hit a classic Guitar Hero pose. He windmilled his arm.

Blang! The lambent chord could have blistered paint.

It still echoed as Harold opened the exit door, stepped through it, and let it shut behind him.

22

Harold turned, but the door through which he'd just stepped was no longer a door. There was nothing but limestone crag, and woods. He held his breath to listen. Nothing.

This way? That way? While deciding, the sound of hooves built. Not galloping; plodding. The creak of wheels and lumber confirmed what Harold suspected.

The wagons with the escaped slaves emerged in front of Harold, who stood in the center of the path. He heard the click of a revolver hammer. Then another, and another. Harriet Tubman ambled out from behind a wagon with her pistol in her hand and regarded Harold.

Out of nowhere, Elizabeth appeared, breathless.

"Harold! Are thou injured or in need of medical assistance?"

Harold raised his arms, palms out. "No."

A voice boomed. "Well, ain't this a sore sight for pleasant eyes!"

Harold saw Daniel on the wagon, fist pumping. Jamal was next to him. Jamal gave vent to his indignation.

"Man, where the fuck you been? Here we are, practically shanghaied, going God knows where in this motherfuckin' horse wagon, eating stuff I never saw before. My stomach hurts, my ass hurts, even my fucking hair hurts."

"What he said," chimed in Daniel, comfortably sprawling in some straw.

Harold took stock and smiled.

"Got room?"

Jamal swung the tailgate down and Harold hitched his butt onto the moving wagon, then climbed aboard. He saw Elizabeth in the wagon in front. She turned to catch his eye, and then turned away. It was the same look he had caught from her out the window of the tour bus.

"Where are we going?" He threw this out as he found a pile of straw to nestle in.

Daniel sighed theatrically and deadpanned, "We're off to see the wizard."

Harold acted the intrigued scholar. "You mean to say, the wonderful Wizard of Oz?"

Jamal's turn. "That's the motherfucker. They say he is a wiz of a wiz if ever a wiz there was."

Harold pulled out his harp and soon the trio began singing the Harold Arlen classic.

"What makes the Hottentots so hot?" Harold shouted.

"Courage!" chorused Daniel and Jamal. They collapsed into giggling like fools.

The slaves looked on with mild interest, loftier issues on their minds. The wagons continued down the track as night began to fall, Harold's harp picking up a new tune.

23

The next day, Harold awoke and was amazed to discover he remained among his companions at a campsite. A fire snapped. Beans and ham hocks for breakfast, after which camp was quickly broken and the caravan got back on track.

The primeval sawtooth ridges of Pennsylvania were merciless. Each mile of crooked, rutted track dodging stone outcroppings and tree obstacles on both sides yielded only to another mile of the same. At times, all aboard needed to step off to lighten the load or push. Inclines were tortuous, and descensions, treacherous.

Two horses suffered broken legs and were put down. Everyone nursed sore type of sore, more than one ache in many cases. Cholera loomed, but never took root. Once in a while, there was water to bathe in and wash clothes, but mostly they all just stunk. They chewed dried meat, drank muddy water, and wiped asses with leaves.

Four days later, they rounded a bend and saw a clearing ahead. In front of them in the path stood three men, each cradling a rifle. Two were black and one white. The white man, a bruiser in buckskin with a beard to the middle of his chest and tangled hair beneath a leather hat with a feather poking out, stepped forward.

"State your business."

The two black men who flanked him were already trading grins with the slaves on the wagons.

Elizabeth dismounted from the buckboard of her wagon and walked up to the man. Harold watched. There was that swagger again, shoulders one way and hips the other. He was a sucker for women who swaggered.

A ceremonial greeting commenced.

"I must first learn to whom I am speaking," Elizabeth said, folding her arms.

"You are speaking to the foreman of this here farm. My name is Hanway."

Elizabeth nodded, satisfied. "Is there a William Parker here? I am given to understand he is expecting our party."

Hanway tipped his hat. "Indeed there is, ma'am. And, indeed he is expecting you."

The acceptance party stepped aside and the wagons rolled forward.

Acres and acres had been cleared on this working farm. The wagons creaked and rumbled through fields planted in corn and beans. Men and women, black and white, wielded hoes against weeds. Others harvested the bounty. The limestone soil, enriched with forest litter and washed free of calcite, had found a worthy partner here.

Children gleaned for remains. One man shouted and the others bellowed back in unison, over and over, rhythmically, a field holler that matched the rise and fall of shoulders and the lifting of hands. The overhead sun steeped the whole scene in energy and serenity.

The wagons rolled up to a two-story house where smoke chugged from dual chimneys. Women carried tubs of laundry into the house. Children were everywhere, one pushing a wheelbarrow by raising his arms over his head. All were dressed in rough homespun.

The front door of the house blew open abruptly and out strode a black man built out of brick. William Parker, free black Pennsylvania planter, abolitionist, and shameless clothes horse. His red flocked vest alone glowed in resplendent glory and his blue frock coat and blue britches, stuffed into knee-high boots, portrayed a man who had been able to bend life's circumstances, however difficult, in his favor.

Parker threw his paws on his hips, arched his back, and let go a horse laugh at the wagons arrayed before him.

"More mischief! More mischief! Mischief keep comin' my way!"

Harriet Tubman was off her wagon and walking up to Parker. They greeted with a hug and then Parker held her at arm's length. "Moses, still parting the waters?"

"No choice. Pharaoh still troubling the people."

They hugged again and walked into the house.

24

Darkness softly inked out the daylight, and Harold sat on a bench on the front porch, rubbing a fresh ankle bruise. Animated voices drifted from inside the house, and he heard the clanking of pots being washed after the roast pork dinner.

Elizabeth approached with a young couple in tow. They wore black clothing, like her, and held hands delicately. They looked at Harold, eyes wide with curiosity. *Munchkins*, Harold thought.

"Harold, this is George and Emily Bradshaw. They are old friends and they live and work here with Mr. Parker."

Harold nodded affably.

"Have thee come a long way?" asked George. Harold wondered what Elizabeth had told them.

"Depends on how you measure that."

"Elizabeth tells us thee came from Maryland. That is close, but the Mason-Dixon line separates the free North from the enslaved South. It can be so distant between the free and the aggrieved who live in bondage."

"Geography's the least of it."

Emily stepped forward and clasped her hands to her bosom. A febrile fervor shone in her eyes.

"Some people live here, others pass through. I judge thee are one who will not stay. This hideous institution of slavery has a way of binding people together who oppose it. Blacks, whites, Quakers, and even Baptists. We are all children in the same light. We may spend our whole lives together or see each other for only a day, but we share something, an earnest embrace of justice and belief in human worth. It's a glowing ember and I have seen it in many."

She took another step forward. "And I see it in thee."

Harold had no words for that.

The couple turned and proceeded into the house and, after a quiet moment, Harold turned to Elizabeth. "Let's go for a walk," he said.

They found a path alongside a murmuring stream.

"I don't know much about Quakers. I think you call yourself the Society of Friends. And you're pacifists."

Elizabeth folded her arms and took a moment to reply. "Among ourselves we say Friends. But we accept being called Quakers, too. That word was used in a condescending manner, but by embracing it we show humility."

"Where is your home?" Harold inquired.

"Philadelphia."

"You have family?"

"My parents are currently in England, raising funds for our struggle. I also have a brother living in Philadelphia who is also raising funds."

"Do you have a husband?"

Elizabeth searched Harold's face intently, then answered.

"The time may come when I wish to marry. I am, at present, involved in work that puts my very life in peril. It is not an opportune time to wed."

"I can see that. As it happens, I am not married either."

Harold stopped walking and turned to face Elizabeth. "How is it in your Society, I mean, between men and women? I mean, are there rules of, um, courtship?"

A smile tweaked a corner of Elizabeth's mouth as she regarded Harold. It was as frank an appraisal as he had ever felt from a woman.

"Friends regard men and women as equals. There are even women leaders of our services. In matters of the heart, all that is required is honesty. If thou are wondering about intimacy, we do not share that promiscuously, but we share it with forthright honesty."

Harold took each of Elizabeth's hands in his and pulled her a little closer. She did not resist, but cocked her head slightly and continued.

"There are times when it is not possible to calculate the depth or worth of one's feelings across the unascertainable measure of our time available. In such times, all that matters is the urgency of the moment. How many of such moments will we have? Only God knows."

"Who knows, indeed, how many such moments." Harold lifted her chin. "I'd like to kiss you."

Elizabeth removed her bonnet and, in a girlish moment, pulled out her combs and shook her hair free. Their kiss was gentle at first, but as Harold felt Elizabeth's hands steal across his shoulders and one hand rest tightly against his neck, he pressed his mouth against her neck. Elizabeth sighed and arched her back. Harold began undoing the buttons on the front of Elizabeth's dress as she held his head in her hands and grinned, welcoming his boldness. Her eyes were wide and she looked at Harold with an almost masculine determination. Elizabeth regarded her womanhood as her gift and she had found the man to whom she wished to give it. Harold kissed her breasts, soft cones pale in the moonlight. The couple sank to their knees and Harold removed his jacket, spreading it on the grass.

Upon removing their clothing, Elizabeth lay on her back on Harold's jacket, legs drawn up. He knelt at her feet as they paused to gaze at each other. Then, she lifted her arms in welcome and enveloped Harold. They began a gentle rocking that ended with little cries from both of them.

The stream beside them gurgled, as streams always do.

25

The sun had been up for an hour and Harold was helping the women clear the breakfast dishes. Jamal stood outside, teaching children a playground game called I Declare War, and Daniel was getting the hang of smoking a clay pipe with some farmhands on the porch.

Distantly, a honking sound arose. Everyone froze. There it was again, a drawn-out blare, echoing across the fields. To Harold, it sounded like a blast one might hear at a hockey game.

The effect was galvanic. Men and women in the fields dropped their tools where they stood and dashed back to the house. The children were gathered up and shooed into the house. Two men began leading animals into the barn.

As the newcomers gathered to puzzle out what was happening, Elizabeth dashed out in a rush, holding up her skirt. She blew stray hair out of her face.

"It's Stoltzfus, our Amish neighbor, issuing a warning. Slavers are coming. Thou should go inside and follow Parker's instructions."

Inside, a defense drill was under way, but this was no drill. Window shutters were closed and furniture was moved to block windows. Parker opened a wall locker, revealing an array of Pennsylvania long rifles and revolvers. He handed out weapons and ammunition. Harold stood, a Paterson Colt in one hand and a fistful of shells in the other.

Footsteps were heard descending the stairs. Harriet Tubman walked in with blood in her eyes as she loaded her revolver. She tucked the gun into her waistband and tied a scarf over her head.

"We might be sending some slavers to heaven today," she said.

"Maybe they deserve worse," Harold said.

"It ain't about what they deserve. They don't know any better. But as long as they crazy, we have to protect ourselves."

Outside, men pushed open the barn doors. Two wagons emerged with the children and women in the back. Elizabeth was at the reins of the first wagon. Harold saw her and bolted out the front door to the road as they passed, running alongside the wagon.

"Where are you going?"

"The Amish farm. We'll be safe there with the children."

Harold stopped running and watched the wagons recede. Elizabeth, her hair still an exploding red mop, turned her head back briefly to Harold and there was that little smile again. Harold's heart leapt before he returned to the house.

26

Men on horseback, carrying an ample amount of rope, charged up the lane, some already with pistols drawn. They were all a-whoop and shouting. Gorsuch led the charge, holding his stovepipe hat on his head by the brim. The posse pulled up in the lane in front of the Parker house and the men dismounted.

Theirs was an exercise in muscle flexing and bull bellowing. Some waved pistols as others pulled carbines from scabbards. A barely disciplined crew of bounty hunters, thrill seekers, and farm hands, they slapped off the dust as they gathered around Gorsuch, who put his hands on his hips while surveying the squinting faces.

He enjoyed having an ardent audience.

"Boys, I reckon you know why we're here. Yonder in that house are four of my slaves, including Amos. Some negresses and pickaninnies, too. I swear before you it is a panorama of stolen merchandise that puts to the test white ownership of negroes."

He slapped fist into palm. "This must not stand!"

One of the men raised a dirt-encrusted finger.

"Am I mistaken, or is anyone we shoot in there a nigger or a nigger lover who is violating the law?"

Gorsuch cleared his throat.

"First off, don't shoot my property. But you'd be doing the law, yourselfs, and me a service if you shoot yourself an abolitionist today." He surveyed the men again. "Y'all take careful aim."

The vigilantes arranged themselves for a siege.

Within the house, Harriet Tubman turned to Amos. "Which one is Gorsuch?" she asked.

"The one running his mouth."

The wail of a harmonica filled the air and the defenders saw Harold seated on the floor with his back against the wall, huffing into the instrument. It was from an Ennio Morricone film score.

Gorsuch walked a few steps toward the house and stopped, pausing to take in the harmonica music.

"Real nice, real nice. Y'all got someone of talent in there." He hooked his thumbs in the armholes of his vest. "Now, y'all know I got me a warrant demanding return of my property, which I can rightfully seize on account of the Fugitive Slave Act." He cleared his throat. "Amos, you in there?"

A moment of silence passed.

"I am here. You and your men best be on your way. None of us are going back to Maryland."

Gorsuch wiped his brow with a rag and pressed on.

"Amos, I promise I won't sell you down the river. I will keep you on my farm and, yes, there'll be a whipping as a lesson to the others. But after that, I'll take your peaceable return, as well as the others, as a sign of good faith and I will not chain you. I swear to the almighty that I will not put shackles upon you."

"Kiss my black ass."

A fierce scowl erupted on the slave owner's face.

"You impudent nigger, you and those others who ran off belong to me, belong to my farm. It is within my rights to take you by force. And that is what me and my men are prepared to do. Right here. Right now."

He turned to his vigilantes, each of whom had guns trained on the house. "Right, boys?"

They whooped in response.

Gorsuch yanked the warrant from inside his vest and thrust it out toward the house.

"This is the warrant signed by a judge. This is the law talkin',
you ungrateful black ass son of a bitch! I own you!"

Inside, Amos thoughtfully worked his tongue against a molar,
his rifle trained on Gorsuch. He turned to Harriet.

"You don't shoot him, I gonna shoot you," he said.

Amos grinned, smacked his lips like he was ready for breakfast,
aimed, and fired. Two holes appeared instantly, one in the warrant and,
behind it, one in Gorsuch's chest. Aghast, Gorsuch's eyes bulged as he
dropped to his knees, clutching the wound, which pumped blood.

"Great God Almighty! Shot by my own nigger!" ✔

Gorsuch fell on his face in the dirt, shuddered once, and remained still.

After a shocked pause, one of the vigilantes screamed and ran
to the prostrate figure.

"Father!" Josh Gorsuch rolled his father over and confronted
the irrefutable evidence of death before him. Josh's rage distorted his
face as he rose to his feet and turned to the Parker house with filial
fury.

"By God, you will pay for this!" Josh aimed his pistol, but before he could fire, a second shot rang out from the house and the Gorsuch offspring fell with a yell of surprise. ✔

Two men from the posse rushed forward, grabbed Josh Gorsuch, and dragged him behind a tree and propped him in a seated position. They hovered over the dying man, whose chest was heaving and
jaw slack. His face twisted.

"Kill them all! After you rape the women, burn the house!
Leave no blade of grass …"

With that, Josh Gorsuch burped up blood, lolled his head, and
ceased to move.

The men straightened uncertainly to consider their next move.

Inside the house, at a window, his smoking rifle still aimed at
the spot where the Gorsuch scion had been in his sights, was Jamal.
He looked around and found the eyes of the others upon him.

"Too bad the Army ain't getting me, huh?"

Then, it was Amos' monster voice again, calling out the window.

"Y'all go home and you will be unmolested. Let us shed no
more blood."

From somewhere among the vigilante crowd, a voice responded. "Molest this, you nigger cocksucker!"

A shot rang out from the lane, a window broke, and splinters flew from an overhead beam. Rifles and pistols roared and gun smoke rose into the trees as a blistering torrent of lead tore through the settlement in every direction.

The glass in the windows of the Parker house disintegrated under the fusillade. Bullets blew up crockery on shelves and riddled metal pots. Debris flew down from blasted brick and wood, inflicting dozens of cuts on the men hunkered below the windows. Each face wore grim determination. Only two outcomes were possible: Drive off the slavers or die.

Harriet Tubman kept her revolver trained on the men in the lane, looking for a target. When one of the men in her sight rose to a standing position to shoot, she fired. The man keeled over with a grunt.

"Lord, accept this miscreant into your kingdom. He was a slaver and a vigilante seeking a bounty, but he knew no better."

She shook her head as she replaced the bullet in the cylinder.

The vigilantes, lying in the tall grass, kept the firepower up, but were effectively pinned down as soil erupted next to them and bullets thudded into the trees overhead.

Two of the men conferred. One, with a leather hat tied under his chin, gestured at the barn with his thumb.

"Smokin' em out's the only way. I'll wager there's kerosene in that barn."

A yellow-toothed grin split the other man's heavy beard. A lunatic gleam shone in his eyes.

"Get ready to cover me."

Leather Hat jammed two fingers in his mouth, giving off a sharp tweet. The others looked at him.

"Get ready for cover fire." He elbowed his bearded cohort, who sprinted toward the barn. "Fire!"

A powerful volley riddled the house in a new eruption of glass and splinters.

Those within the house dove for whatever cover remained. Somebody screamed in pain. Dense gun smoke floated in layers inside a house now devoid of yesterday's repose.

The vigilante darted inside the barn and soon returned swinging a galvanized can on a handle, keeping outside the line of fire. He approached a shed attached to the house and climbed on top. Now he could reach the roof, which was level with his chin. He pushed the can onto the roof, then took a grip on the edge, and pushed up. He attempted to get a leg up when a shot rang out. He fell back onto the shed roof, then toppled to the ground with a thud.

The shot came from the roof itself, where two women, both black and holding rifles, sat on the shakes behind a cornice hiding them from view.

Inside, Harriet had seen the man fall past a window. She shook her head. "Mmm. Mmm. Mmm."

The women on the roof crawled to the peak, where they could peer over at the lane. They leveled their rifles at the vigilantes, who were in plain view from above, and opened fire.

The men in the lane sought better cover.

"Fuck this," one declared, in a tone of exasperation, holstering his gun and bolting for his horse. His retreat spurred a panicked rush for the horses as the siege caved.

Parker, his white shirt stained with blood from cuts, turned to the others inside. "Men, you may stop shooting. The day is ours. Judgment still awaits those cowards who flee, but not today."

Harriet returned her pistol to a pocket on her dress. "Once again, instead of reaping crops, we reap dead men. God give me strength."

A cry of dismay erupted from the next room and the crowd rushed in, gathering around the corpse of Daniel Bodine, sprawled on the floor atop of his rifle. He'd been shot through the heart. His face wore the expression of surprise at greeting eternity.

Jamal threw his hands to his face and quaked with shock, then turned away. Harold rolled his eyes upward and slammed his fist against his thigh. The others looked on, faces heavy with pity and grief.

Shaking his head and grimacing, Parker put on his hat and headed for the door. "I'm going to Stoltzfus's to give the all clear," he said, voice a choke.

27

On a rise near the house, on land cleared for a cemetery, mourners lowered their heads around an open grave. A body wrapped in a clean white sheet lay next to it.

Jamal lifted his head and sighed. "I wish my grandmother from Baltimore was here. She'd know what to say." He paused and shook his head as if in disbelief. "Here was a man. A man who will be missed, who I called a friend. He was a soldier who fought for peace. Y'all might say, 'What? A soldier for peace?' Well, he went to Vietnam a soldier for war and came back a soldier for peace. Maybe even a soldier for revolution. If you don't get that, I can't explain it. Danny boy, Semper Fi."

He opened his fist to reveal Daniel's dog tags, which he draped on a wood cross at one end of the grave. On the cross was inscribed, "Daniel Bodine, soldier."

The sun was setting as they carefully lowered the precious sheeted parcel into the freshly dug grave.

28

At dawn, a rucksack hit the porch, landing next to two others. Harold appeared next to them, followed by Elizabeth and Jamal. Behind them, the sounds of hammers and saws.

Everyone gathered around their packs until Parker came out onto the porch, now in a tartan vest over a white shirt with sleeves rolled to the elbows. The man dealt pragmatically in a world of danger. Best have lots of vests.

Parker surveyed the now-quiet lane in front of his house, then turned his imperious scrutiny to the rucksacks.

"All things diverge here."

"Where's Harriet?" Harold asked.

"She gone. She and Amos headed northbound with the rest of their crew. But she'll be back in time with another crew in tow."

Jamal scratched his chin stubble.

"Change is coming, you best believe. No more parley, just a demand. Without a demand, nothing is given, according to Frederick Douglass."

"A scholar among us," Harold said.

"Mrs. Henderson, eleventh grade American History, City College High School in Baltimore."

Parker wiped his brow. A warm day lay ahead and ample work remained. Running off to abolitionist travel adventures was a lure that appealed to him deeply. But his mission was tied to this farm. This soil.

He turned to Harold, Jamal, and Elizabeth, who were shrugging on their rucksacks and handed Harold a compass. "Keep aiming east on the wagon track," Parker said. "You got four or five days walking. Sorry, but I can't spare horses for you. You'll up and come into the west part of Philadelphia and folks will show you the way from there."

The trio stepped onto the lane, turned left, and commenced their journey. Once, Harold would insist that keeping his corporeal presence above the dirt was a priority. Now, the earth he strode upon in Pennsylvania pointed him in a new direction. He had learned not to concern himself with the destination.

Beneath their feet was the limestone and dolomite, perhaps, deep down, even anthracite, of Pennsylvania bedrock. In the layer above was the debris and soil that gave rise to the ever-present hemlocks, along with maples, ashes, cedars, and assorted pines. The tree canopy was so dense, little undergrowth showed beneath. Rock obstacles, not shrubs, created a minefield of stumble.

The three pilgrims emerged into a clearing. Harold held his hand up to signal a rest. Too tired to speak, he let the pack fall from his shoulders onto the sparse ferns at his feet. Harold sat and propped his back on a rock as his lungs heaved, slowly gained back spent oxygen. The others did likewise.

Jamal was first to break the silence.

"I'm seeing a whole lot of nothing. Where in the hell are we?"

Elizabeth had found burrs in her hair and was removing them. "We're in William Penn's territory, west of Philadelphia. The Society of Friends is there and they will give us succor when we arrive."

"Sucker?"

Harold butted in. "The question is not just where, but when? When we find Philadelphia, *when* will it be? Are we gonna shake hands with Ben Franklin or watch the Eagles in a sports bar?"

The others stared at him but hadn't the strength to question his meaning.

The sky darkened and a rumble of thunder abruptly changed the agenda. Harold got to his feet, grimaced as he arched his back, and looked straight up. There were only trees. Another rumble cracked the darkening sky.

"We best spend the night here. Let's get out the tent."

29

In the thick timber of eastern Pennsylvania, when lightning spidered across a dark, unsettled sky–followed by cannon fire thunder–all animals retreated to ground. The pealing was far and near, and a ruthless wind whipped the trees.

The storm began in earnest.

Rain lashed everything. The little tent shuddered in the gusts. Inside, a flash of lightning illuminated three figures wrapped in blankets, wincing at the fury just beyond the sheet of canvas above them.

No sleep tonight.

Jamal drew his hand down his jaw.

"I used to like storms like this, but that's when I was in my house in west Baltimore. My mama would make bean soup with ham hocks and we'd all huddle in the kitchen and be all nervous and shit, with all the thunder and lightning. But there momma'd be, humming away and stirring her soup. Dad be doing shots of George Dickel while momma shot eye daggers at him. He'd wink at us and say, 'Don't be scared. It just be loud. Ain't no harm.'"

Harold got out his harmonica, tested it, then blew a few notes, the opening bars of something known only to him. He stopped and froze. They all heard it.

Hoofbeats.

Harold stashed the harp and he and Jamal both pulled pistols from rucksacks. Their nerves were drumhead taut.

Elizabeth bowed her head and prayed.

The hoofbeats were now right outside their tent. Guttural male voices were incomprehensible. Harold pulled back the hammer on his revolver and moved to open the buttoned entrance to the tent.

Clank!

A grappling hook hit the tent and tore through the canvas tent. Fabric ripped apart as the hook sliced through the shelter until it caught on a tentpole. Within seconds, the whole tent vanished, hauled upward and outward, leaving Harold, Jamal, and Elizabeth agape in the pelting rain. A man on horseback rode a short distance away, dragging the tent behind. He lifted the rope loop off his pommel and returned to the scene.

He held a pistol on the trio, as did the other two men astride horses and covered with ponchos.

"Aim at the woman!" he barked.

The man who dragged the tent took charge. He lifted his pistol and pointed it straight at Harold's head. "Drop those Colts or die right now. Her first. Live or die."

Jamal tossed his pistol aside. Harold hesitated and was shot in the right arm. His pistol fell to the ground. Elizabeth gasped and flung herself in front of him.

The man on horseback who had fired turned to his compatriots as his horse pedaled a bit. "Did I not warn him? Did I not?"

They nodded. Yes, plenty of warning.

Jamal dashed to Harold's aid, trying to remove Harold's hand from the wounded arm so he could take a look.

The shooter vigilante gave his pistol a vainglorious spin and holstered it. The rain diminished, and he pushed back the hood on his poncho before turning to his friends.

"I'd a shot the nigger, but he's worth more in one piece when we get back to Maryland. As far as this nigger-lovin' abolitionist, there'll be cheers when we get back and they see him flappin' one wing."

The other two chuckled.

Elizabeth, still wrapped in her blanket, rose to her feet, wrath blazing on her face as the rain plastered the hair on her brow.

"Thou are black-hearted men and rank cowards. God gave you souls and gave you the Earth. But thou have forsaken the divine and embraced the unholy. Thou are men, but thy belief in most heinous slavery has driven thee to the level of beasts."

They regarded Elizabeth and her insults as nothing to take seriously. The men smiled as one took a bottle from a saddlebag and gulped a deep swig. He tossed it to another, who wiped the mouth of the bottle and also poured some down his throat.

Elizabeth wasn't finished. She lowered her face like a judge delivering a dire sentence as her voice dropped to a hoarse alto.

"Deep inside thee is a human heart. Cannot thee make peace with us on this wretched night and let us go our way? I cannot guarantee the consequences if thee refuse."

The vigilante with the bottle shoved a cork into it, burped loudly, then wiped his mouth.

"Squawk all you want, ma'am, but we have the law on our side."

"That which is unjust can never survive as law. This Fugitive Slave Act is a covenant with Satan and a pact made in Hell!"

Elizabeth now stood directly in front of the bottle-holder's horse. The horse shifted hooves nervously. More rumbling emerged from the distance. It grew louder.

Harold and Jamal were transfixed as Elizabeth held the stage with cold fury.

"You give me no choice," she said.

Elizabeth removed the blanket from her shoulders and threw it on top of the horse's head; it covered everything from the neck of the horse to its nostrils. The animal snorted softly.

For a moment, nothing happened. The man with the bottle looked perplexed as he gazed down on the blanket-draped creature he was astride. The horse stood placidly.

A rumble built, and then, like blitzkrieg, lightning hit the trees overhead.

The blast stunned the senses of all sentient beings in the vicinity, ripping up auditory sensation, freezing the blood, and triggering panic.

But a stunned silence it was not to be.

A flaming tree branch hurtled downward, slapping off other branches in an incendiary high-five.

Madness!

The three horses shrieked in terror and reared up. The man with the bottle was thrown from his saddle, but his boot and spur caught in the stirrup and, as he slammed into the ground, he was abruptly hauled violently along the left side of his horse. Charging with ungovernable terror through the thick woods, the horse demon swung sharply to the right, bringing the passenger flying wildly against a tree with a rib-busting thud. The boot and spur, stuck in the stirrup, flew off his foot as the horse, now free of its burden, charged off.

The man had no future in events that would ensue.

As the other two vigilantes struggled to control their steeds, Elizabeth grabbed the shirt fronts of Harold and Jamal.

"We must run now."

Jamal found his Colt where he tossed it and the three sprinted out of the clearing into the tree line, Harold holding his bleeding arm as Elizabeth sought to support him. They ran, stumbled, and dodged in a downhill direction.

They could hear the pounding hooves of the two vigilantes behind them. Then, the sound grew intermittent. The reason was clear. The Pennsylvania woods gave no quarter. Between the limestone spurs higher than a man, sudden sinkholes, and tree branches that whipped the face mercilessly, the path, even downhill, was a tortuous game of maneuvering around obstacles.

Harold could feel the blood drip from his fingers holding his ripped arm as the three clambered through a torturous landscape that snagged at clothing and scraped flesh. As treacherous it was for those on foot, it was worse for men on horseback, who sawed at the reins to keep their frightened mounts from plunging into a hole or crashing into a tree.

The three tried to stay together during this agonizing plunge. Through his pain, a thought occurred to Harold that all the tennis training in the world was useless if you couldn't grip a revolver because your hands were too bloody.

Elizabeth kept a grip on Harold's waist as she led the way. Her legs somehow found the footing she needed to descend this ragged and merciless ridge. A savageness filled her. Her dress was in shreds and the branches that swatted her face had drawn blood. One eye was filling with blood, so she kept it shut and powered through with the other.

Jamal picked up the rear. His Colt was out and kept pace, but it was clear exhaustion was imminent. His chest heaved and the rawness of his drawing breath was loud. Desperation pumped his adrenaline, but the high octane of the panic hormone was draining away. He neared the end of his reserve.

The three broke through a dense copse and collapsed on cleared, level ground.

They gathered themselves up and took stock, standing on a track next to a stream, which burbled, serenely and absurdly. Harold looked at his wounded arm, which was leaking blood still, albeit slower. It occurred to him to issue some kind of command, but Elizabeth seized the moment.

"We must flee now on this path. We have no choice."

They ran, Harold staggering, along the cleared space next to the stream. Harold wondered vaguely who cleared this path and when, but Elizabeth tugged him forward and he dismissed that thought for study later.

Jamal ran a few yards behind, checking over his shoulder. He saw the vision they had feared.

Down the path, where they had emerged, two horsemen crashed through the trees to the path and reckoned with their location. It took only a moment for them to spot their quarry one hundred yards ahead, turn their horses, and spur the exhausted and bleeding beasts into a gallop.

The duo who slapped their horses' reins were two hurtling madmen, human spurring equine. The horses had purchase now and room ahead and could be spurred. Hooves thundered, tearing apart the mossy berm beside the stream as they picked up speed. The men, whipping the reins from one side to the other, had eyes fixed straight ahead. In those eyes, blood.

The gap between predator and prey narrowed swiftly. Jamal, drawing ragged breaths as the last of his strength left him, and unable to recover from a stumble, collapsed atop the path. He summoned enough grit to lift the Colt as the hellions bore down on him and, an animal cry in his throat, he swung the gun, now in both hands, in their direction and squeezed the trigger. The weapon blasted out six bullets as he continued to fire until the chamber was empty, which was also the moment the horses thundered over him, a hoof landing a blow alongside his head.

Jamal spun to the ground and was still.

One of the vigilantes slumped in his saddle and clutched his chest. He collapsed, causing the maddened beast beneath him to swerve toward the stream. The man was upended, flung in a vertical rotation—legs up, arms out—until his body hit a tree and did a wicked spin. He landed in a shallow pool with a splash.

30

Harold was groggy now. He felt drained of every-
thing necessary for mind and body to function at a basic level. Contin-
ual forward motion seemed a pathetic waste of what little energy remained. Only Elizabeth's unrelenting grip around his ribs kept him
upright.

Elizabeth spotted a shallow depression under a jutting outcrop
of stone. It was not even a cave, but it was all the shelter they had and
she hustled both of them into it. She had to shove Harold's head down
to prevent it from hitting a low-hanging outcropping.

They slumped against the rear of the stone pocket and Elizabeth pulled Harold into her arms. Harold blinked fast, dimly trying to
make sense out of what seemed senseless. *Why,* he wondered, *do my eyes
seem unable to focus?* He shook his head to clear the fuzz, but it didn't
work. He tried to lift an arm. He succeeded, but his consciousness was
dropping into a well.

He gathered in a huge sigh and let it out. *Oh well, what the hell.
Why am I not dead already? Something is improbable there. Here's this*

woman in a black dress, with a passionate political temperament and strong arms, and those arms are around me now. He'd forgotten his own arm with the hole in it. He turned his head forward, to the entrance of their little stone shelter, and his eyes seemed to focus better.

Elizabeth's voice was hoarse at his ear.

"This may be the last time I am able to speak to thee. I want thee to know thou has a place in my heart. I have given my devotion to thee and thou have taken that with the grace of a man with noble intentions in his heart. I know this to be true."

She gripped him tighter around the ribs and the heat of something bloody, anguished and eternal, flooded Harold's body. Death brought no fear now; only separation from this fierce Valkyrie could bring him to bitter tears.

They heard a horse drawing up nearby, followed by a man dismounting.

Soon, a figure loomed before them, lazily swinging a Colt by his side. He was in no hurry and used a fingernail to pick at his teeth as he regarded the two gasping, bleeding renegades. He wore a sweat-soaked flannel shirt beneath buckskin, had a leather thong tied around his neck, and his greasy shoulder-length hair was covered by no hat. He arched his back theatrically.

"Wheeyew!" he started in. "That was some bonus! Y'all got some grit, I will say that. No doubt whatsoever that you sell it dearly. No doubt. But what do I own here? Fact of the matter is, however, that your worth to me as abolitionists, should I bring back to Maryland, could be measured in pig shit as far as bounty is concerned. And I ain't got the time or inclination to …"

He lifted his pistol and cocked it with an almost tired indifference. Just a bitter end to a bitter story he will tell in Maryland.

With a sucking sound, an arrow pierced the would-be assassin's neck. The bloody front of the arrow was visible directly out of his Adam's apple.

The vigilante opened his mouth in a failed, desperate attempt to speak. He lifted a hand and gripped the protruding arrow extending outward from the front of his neck but was unable to determine what to do with it. Stupidly, he just held it as blood poured out and his eyes bugged.

He turned around in hopes of solving this puzzle, which exposed his chest, and with another hissing sound a second arrow found its mark, this one piercing his rib cage and protruding just south of his left armpit.

The dying man held both arrows in his hands now as he crashed to the ground. His collapse revealed a figure at the entrance to their cave, a figure holding a bow.

The Indian gazed impassively at the twice-impaled man, now motionless on the forest floor. He glanced abstractedly at Elizabeth and Harold, who could only goggle in astonishment. The Indian mounted his horse and, signaling to his companion, the two turned their horses and rode off.

Harold had no wit left to process all this and could only fall back into Elizabeth's enfolding arms. She buried her face in Harold's neck and sobbed. Harold lifted his head and gazed at the dark rock surrounding them and wondered what fresh hell would appear in the gap next.

Footsteps.

Someone walked unsteadily nearby. Harold could hear heavy breathing and Elizabeth lifted her head. This apparition had a name, and Harold was filled with elation because it was a name he knew.

Jamal appeared at the mouth of the little cave and let out a ragged breath as he regarded the two of them huddled inside. He held a cloth against his bleeding forehead. He looked down at the arrow-pierced miscreant on the forest floor and rolled his eyes, as if attempting to solve a puzzle that had no solution in a sane world. His teeth chattered, but he looked outward to take in the thick aggregation of woods that surround them.

"Sick of these fucking trees," he said.

He picked up a rock and flung it, bouncing it off a pine.

The Pennsylvania woods were indifferent to his words.

At the top of the pine, a crow lifted off and lazily flapped its wings. This was corvine territory. Crows owned all that was below, even though other creatures might pass through. High atop the trees, they kept an eye out.

31

One woman and two men emerged from the woods in daylight under placid clouds and found themselves on a rutted lane that led, judging by the sun, eastward. They walked gingerly, in no particular hurry.

One of the men, who was white, had his arm in a sling and used a branch as a walking stick. A woman in a tattered black dress walked next to him with a rucksack slung over one shoulder. Her eyes strafed the woods around them, alert for any menace.

In front strode a black man, white bandanna around his head, still showing a blood stain, revolver in hand, eyeballs restive in their sockets. He remembered the term "itchy trigger finger." Yeah, that about summed it up. His thumb caressed the Colt's hammer.

A sound behind them hit their radar. Wagon wheels and horses' hooves grew closer. A wagon drawn by two horses emerged from the woods onto the track. Two men sat on the buckboard.

The trio halted at the approach of the wagon, and Jamal tucked the pistol into his waistband and covered it out of prudent caution.

The wagon trundled up and Harold examined the faces of the two bearded men, who were dressed in homespun.

"Max and Benny," Harold said.

The two men on the wagon looked him over. "It's that ragamuffin again," Benny said, snorting with laughter. "He keeps turning up like a bad penny. Can't spend him, but you don't want to throw him away."

Harold clasped his hands and held them at his waist.

"I hope I have earned your trust, because we could use your help," he said.

Max took a pipe from his mouth, spat, and said, "You've always dealt plain with us, poor miserable cuss that you are."

Max then elbowed Benny.

"Miserable fucking cuss," Benny added.

The two waggoneers snickered wetly.

"We could use a ride, if you could see your way," Harold said.

"Which way?"

Elizabeth stepped forward. "We are bound for Philadelphia. We hope to rendezvous with William Penn himself."

"Can't say I've met the man," Benny offered. "You folks are vagabonds, and I have two questions for vagabonds. Do any of you have the cholera?"

The three shook their heads.

"Are you armed?"

Jamal lifted the Colt from his waistband.

"I'd be obliged if you let us hold that," Benny said.

"Ain't gonna happen." Jamal tucked the weapon back in his waistband.

Max took the pipe from his mouth, snorted back a volume of phlegm, and swallowed.

Harold intervened. "Max, Benny, we are no threat to you. One of us is armed for protection because otherwise we come through dangerous territory in a helpless condition."

Elizabeth walked up and held forth. "We are abolitionists doing God's work. The total immolation of slavery is our goal. So fierce is our devotion to this mission that our very bodies and souls are held together for its completion."

She took a place beside Harold. "Look at this man. Just look. He has suffered grievously since taking up our mission. Thou should take pity."

She walked up to the wagon and placed her hand over the reins.

"We may appear like the basest of wretches to you. But I say to you now that all I suffer in privation and destitution is to one purpose, that God grant that my eyes can behold the destruction of human bondage before my body is given over to the worms. I swear this to be truly my mission!" Elizabeth thought a moment, then added, "*Our* mission!"

Max and Benny exchanged a glance.

Max shoved the pipe back into his mouth. "Got any money to pay us?" he asked.

"We have nothing to offer you," Elizabeth said, "except the satisfaction that accrues from aiding a divine mission."

Max gave that some thought. "We ain't so divine in our mission, ma'am. See those jugs in the wagon? That was apple cider, but now it's fairly hard jack. Get you cross-eyed in a fiddler's wink."

Jamal's eyes lit up. "Sounds pretty fucking divine to me."

Harold, also smacking his lips, just told it.

"You know me. We all go back a long way, Max and Benny. A long goddamn way. I was one ragamuffin. Now we're three ragamuffins and we could use a ride."

One of the horses began shaking its head.

"Where you headed again?" Benny asked.

"Philadelphia," Elizabeth answered.

"We can get you partway there. Get in," Max said. "Just don't suck down all our jack."

The three clambered into the back of the wagon.

The wagon lurched forward as the horses took to their harnesses again with a squeak of leather. Elizabeth sat with her back against the rack of jugs, spread her legs, and gathered Harold by the armpits until he was leaning back against her. Harold winced, cradling his arm.

"Fix you up," Jamal said, as he sat next to Elizabeth. He passed the Colt to Harold, who held it in his lap, and lifted a jug. He took a long swig and passed the jug to Harold.

"Some serious shit here," Jamal said, coughing. "God bless Johnny Appleseed."

Harold wrestled the heavy jug to his mouth and let the fiery

apple brandy flow down his gullet. He knew better than to offer any
to Elizabeth. He lifted the jug once more, and water sprang from his
eyes as more of the jack went down. But he felt a blanket of comfort
that diminished his pain a bit. Harold sighed and passed the jug back
to Jamal.

The wagon emerged from the rutted path onto a ramp that led
to a paved eastbound lane that led to a paved ramp and onto a modern
highway. The wagon's ironclad wheels made a racket on the asphalt
roadbed.

Traffic passed them, including a yellow school bus full of children who pressed their faces against the window to puzzle over this
antique horse-drawn buckboard with worse-for-wear passengers, one
of them holding a gun.

Harold waved at them and the children eagerly waved back.
One of the boys held up his index finger and blew imaginary smoke
from his fingertip. Harold winked back at the boy.

A cherry red 1957 Chevrolet Belair raced by in the opposite
direction. Harold just caught a glimpse as the bus pulled ahead of the
wagon. He smiled and pulled out his harmonica and tested it in his
good hand. He watched the highway recede behind him, as crows
soared overhead.

DAVID STURM

David Sturm, a Baltimore native, is a retired newspaper reporter who currently lives in Silver Spring, Maryland. He has written three movie screenplays, and WELCOME TO BREEZEWOOD is his first novel. David is married and has a son and a daughter.

Joe

Made in the USA
Middletown, DE
10 August 2019